This Book belongs to:

....

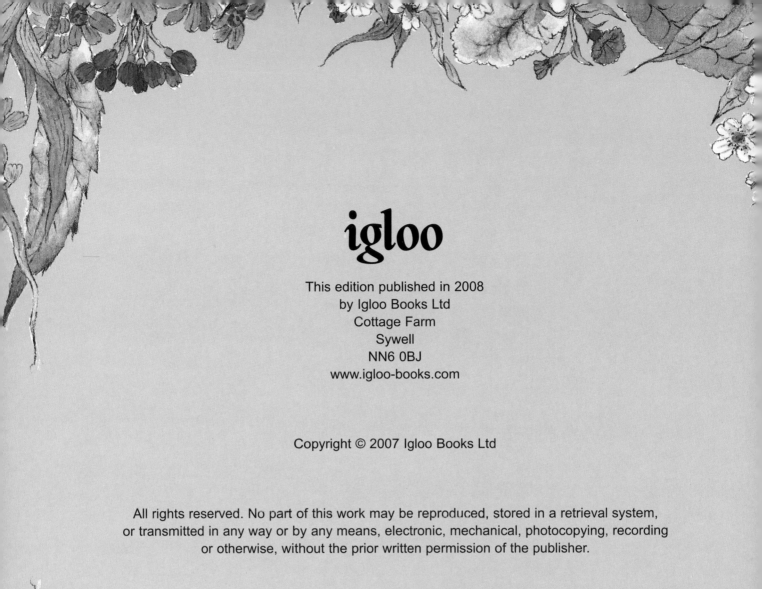

igloo

This edition published in 2008
by Igloo Books Ltd
Cottage Farm
Sywell
NN6 0BJ
www.igloo-books.com

10 9 8 7 6 5 4 3 2

ISBN: 978 1 8456 1778 3

Project Managed by Page to Page
Designed by Chris Fraser

Printed and manufactured in China

My Treasury
of
Fairy Tales

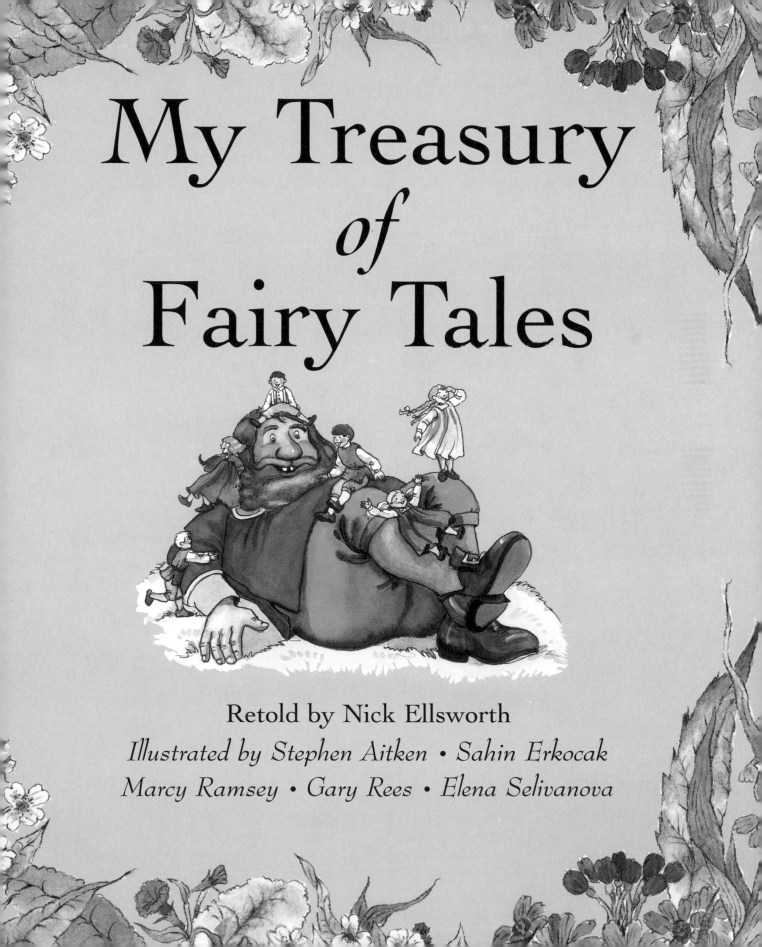

Retold by Nick Ellsworth

Illustrated by Stephen Aitken • Sahin Erkocak
Marcy Ramsey • Gary Rees • Elena Selivanova

Contents

For Younger Children

For Older Children

Goldilocks and The Three Bears

Once upon a time there was a lovely little cottage that sat right in the middle of the woods. In this cottage lived a family of friendly bears. There was Big Papa Bear, who could be a little grumpy at times, Medium-sized Mama Bear, who was just as a mother should be and Teenie Weenie Baby Bear, who liked to play all day.

One fine day they all stomped down to the kitchen for their usual breakfast of delicious homemade porridge. Papa Bear ate his porridge out of a big bowl, Mama Bear ate her porridge out of a medium-sized bowl, while Teenie Weenie Baby Bear had his very own teenie weenie bowl.

Papa Bear scooped up a large spoonful of porridge and popped it straight into his mouth. "Ouch," he cried. "That's too hot!" Mama Bear tasted hers. "Ooh, I suppose it is a bit hot," she agreed.
"It will burn my mouth!" cried Teenie Weenie Baby Bear after tasting his.

"I've got a good idea," said Mama Bear. "Why don't we go for a walk in the woods? By the time we get back, our porridge will be cool."
"Oh, all right," said Papa Bear a bit grumpily. He really would have liked to go back to bed until his porridge cooled down.
"Yippee!" yelled Teenie Weenie Baby Bear. "I can show you how fast I can run."
So, shutting the door behind them, the three bears went for a walk in the woods.

Not long after they had gone, a little girl called Goldilocks, who was out walking in the woods, stumbled across the little cottage where the three bears lived. She thought it was so lovely that she wanted to look inside. She carefully opened the door and shut it quietly behind her.

The first thing she noticed were the three bowls of porridge on the kitchen table.

"They look really yummy," she thought. "I'm so hungry. I'm sure no one would mind if I ate just a little."

First, she tried a spoonful of porridge from the big bowl. But that was too salty.

Next, she tried a spoonful of porridge from the medium-sized bowl. But that was too sweet.

Finally, she tried a spoonful of porridge from the teenie weenie bowl. That was just right. Goldilocks was so hungry she ate every last bit. She felt tired after eating so much and decided to sit down for a while.

First, she tried to sit in a big chair but it was so big, her feet didn't even touch the ground.

Next, she tried a medium-sized chair. That was a little better but she could only reach the ground with her toes.

Finally, she sat in a teenie weenie chair and that was just right. But she was far too big for the teenie weenie chair and, when she sat down in it, she broke it!

"I wonder if there are any beds upstairs," she thought. "I'm sure no one would mind if I lay down for a while."

She went upstairs and saw three beds.

The first bed she tried was a big, floppy bed. "This bed is far too soft," she thought.

The next bed was a very neat, medium-sized bed. "This bed is far too hard," she thought.

Finally, she lay on a teenie weenie bed. "This bed is just right," thought Goldilocks, and was soon fast asleep.

When the three bears returned from their walk, they were very hungry and looking forward to eating their porridge. The first thing they saw were the spoons lying in the porridge bowls.

"Who's been eating my porridge?" cried Papa Bear in a big, grumpy voice.

"Who's been eating my porridge?" cried Mama Bear in a medium-sized voice.

"Who's been eating my porridge, and eaten it all up?" cried Teenie Weenie Baby Bear in a teenie weenie voice.

Papa Bear was so grumpy he decided to have a sit down, but noticed that the cushion on his chair was messed up.

"Who's been sitting in my chair?" he cried in his big, grumpy voice.

"Who's been sitting in my chair?" cried Mama Bear in her medium-sized voice, noticing that her cushion was messed up, too.

"And who's been sitting in my chair and broken it?" yelled Teenie Weenie Baby Bear in his teenie weenie voice.

"This is making me really grumpy," said Papa Bear in his big, grumpy voice. "I'm going to bed." The other bears agreed and followed him up the stairs.

When they got there, they saw that their beds had been messed up, too.
"Who's been sleeping in my bed?" cried Papa Bear in his big, grumpy voice.
"Who's been sleeping in my bed?" cried Mama Bear in her medium-sized voice.
"And who's been sleeping in my bed, and is still sleeping in my bed?" cried Teenie Weenie Baby Bear in his teenie weenie voice.

All this shouting woke Goldilocks. When she saw the three bears looking down angrily at her, she leaped out of bed, ran down the stairs, out the door and into the woods as fast as she could. And the three bears were very pleased that they never saw her, ever again.

Jack and The Beanstalk

Jack lived with his mother in an old cottage in a field. They were very poor. The only thing they owned was a cow called Milky-white. One day, poor old Milky-white stopped giving them milk. "You'd better take her to the market and sell her," Jack's mother told him. "At least we'll be able to buy some bread and honey with the money we get for her."

The next morning, Jack and Milky-white set out bright and early on the road to the market. Halfway there, Jack noticed an old man sitting at the side of the road.
"Fine morning," said Jack.
"It certainly is," said the man. "What a fine looking cow you have there."
"I'm taking her to the market to sell her," replied Jack.
"Perhaps you would sell her to me," said the old man. "I have no money, but I do have five magic beans I could give you."

Jack thought this was a very fair exchange. After saying goodbye to Milky-white, he put the magic beans safely in his pocket and ran home to his mother. When he'd told her what had happened and showed her the magic beans, she was furious with him.
"You stupid boy," she said. "You may as well have given our cow away. Now, we have nothing to eat and no money to buy any food. Go to your room at once!"
Then she threw the beans out the window.

When Jack woke up the next morning, there was a strange shadow over his bed. He looked out the window and couldn't believe his eyes. Overnight, one of the beans had grown into a huge beanstalk. It was so big, he couldn't see the top. It just disappeared into the clouds.

Jack stepped out his window onto the beanstalk and started to climb. He went higher and higher until he couldn't see the ground at all. At the very top, was a rough track. He followed the track until he came to a huge castle. He walked around the castle walls until he came to a great door. He crept inside and found himself inside an immense kitchen.

Suddenly, he came face to face with an enormous woman.
"Ah, a little boy," she said. "My husband loves to eat little boys for breakfast. Lucky for you, I've already made him breakfast today."
Suddenly, Jack heard footsteps. They were so loud, they shook the whole castle.
"Quick, hide!" said the enormous woman.

"That's my husband coming. He'll want to eat you if he sees you."
Jack hid among the gigantic pots and pans and saw a great big giant enter the kitchen. He sang a strange song in a big, rumbling voice.

"Fee, fi, fo, fum.
I smell the blood of an Englishman.
Be he alive or be he dead,
I'll grind his bones to make my bed."

Jack had never been so frightened in his life. He kept as still as possible. Hiding behind the pots and pans, he watched as the giant sat down at a vast table and ate a huge breakfast of eggs, bacon and toast. After he'd finished eating, he pulled a bag of gold coins from his pocket and began to count them. The giant got halfway through counting the coins, before he leaned back in his chair and fell fast asleep. His snoring sounded like the rumble of thunder.

Jack carefully slipped out from his hiding place, tucked two of the huge gold coins under his arm, and quickly ran out of the castle and back to the beanstalk. He threw the coins down to his garden and climbed down as fast as he could.

When he reached the bottom, he found his mother staring in amazement at the gold coins. When Jack told her his astonishing story, his mother couldn't help but believe him. The proof was right there in front of her: the two gold coins.

For the next few months, Jack and his mother had everything they wanted. They bought all the food they could eat and furnished their cottage from top to bottom. But, soon, the money ran out and Jack realized that he'd have to get more. So, up the beanstalk he went again. When he got to the kitchen this time, he hid in the massive oven. Just in time, because the ground began to shake as the giant stomped in for breakfast.

"Fee, fi, fo, fum.
I smell the blood of an Englishman.
Be he alive or be he dead,
I'll grind his bones to make my bed."

The giant sat down with a great thump and, like the last time, was served an enormous breakfast by his enormous wife. After he'd finished, he put a hen on the table.
"Oh, no. He's not going to eat that, too," thought Jack from his hiding place.
But the giant didn't eat it. He just roared, "Lay!" to the hen, and the hen laid a golden egg!
A few minutes later, the giant roared "Lay!" to the hen again. It laid another golden egg!
"I must have that hen," thought Jack. When the giant was sleeping, he sneaked out of the oven, grabbed the hen and ran as fast as he could to the beanstalk.

At the bottom, Jack's mother was astonished when she saw the hen lay-
ing golden eggs, and gave Jack a great big hug. Jack became very rich.
But he soon got bored having nothing to do, so he climbed the beanstalk
once again.

When he reached the castle this time, he hid in the log basket. As usual,
the giant ate his huge breakfast. When he'd finished, he put a little harp
on the table.

"Play!" roared the giant. The harp began to play the most beautiful
music.

"I must have that harp," thought Jack. After the giant had fallen asleep,
Jack climbed out of the log basket, snatched the harp from the table
and ran out of the castle.

But the harp cried, "Help me, master! Help me, master!"

The giant woke with a start and, when he realized what was happening, chased Jack all the way to the beanstalk. Jack threw the harp down, and then began to climb down himself. Looking up, he saw that the giant was climbing down after him! The beanstalk was shaking and waving around under the giant's huge weight.

When Jack got to the bottom, he grabbed an axe and quickly chopped down the beanstalk. The giant came crashing to the ground and was killed at once.

There were no more adventures for Jack and his beanstalk. The harp was broken but Jack and his mother still had the hen that laid golden eggs, so they never had to worry about anything ever again, and lived happily ever after.

Puss in Boots

There was once a miller who had three sons. When the miller died, he left all he had to his three boys. To the eldest son, he left the mill, to the middle son, he left his donkey and, to the youngest son, he left his cat.

The youngest son wasn't very happy about this at all.
"That's not fair," he moaned. "You can make money if you've got a mill, and you can make money if you've got a donkey. But how can I make money if I've only got a cat?"
"Don't worry, master," said Puss. "You won't have to worry about anything. Just do as I ask."

Puss asked his master to bring him a sack and a pair of boots to wear. Puss put on the boots and walked around proudly in them. "I look very fine in these," he thought. Then he put some barley into the sack with some fresh green leaves, and left the sack in the middle of a field. After a while, lured by the delicious smell, some curious rabbits made their way into the sack, hoping for a bit of a feast. Puss, who had been hiding nearby, quickly pounced on top of the sack and tied up the top. The rabbits were trapped inside.

Puss then walked up to the castle where the King lived.
"I'd like to see the King," he said boldly to the sentry guard who was on duty.

"Who shall I say wishes to see the King?" asked the sentry.
"I am the servant of the Marquis of Carabas," said Puss.

Once inside the castle, the cat offered the sack of rabbits to the King.
"These are for you, your Majesty. A present from my master, the
Marquis of Carabas."
The clever puss was pretending that his real master, the miller's son, was
a nobleman!
"How nice," said the King. "Rabbit is delicious in a stew. Please thank
your master for me."

A few days later, Puss caught some partridges in the sack and gave them to the King.

"Partridge is wonderful when it's roasted," said the King. "Please pass my warmest regards on to your master."

The next day, Puss had heard that the King's carriage was going to drive along a road running close to a river. Puss told the miller's son to take all his clothes off and jump into the water. By now, the miller's son realised that his cat was no ordinary cat, and decided to do whatever he asked. Puss quickly hid his master's clothes behind a rock.

When the King's carriage passed by, Puss leapt out in front of it, shouting, "Help! My master, the Marquis of Carabas, is drowning!" The King ordered his carriage to stop and told his servants to help the miller's son out of the river.

"My dear Marquis," said the King. "What a terrible thing to happen. You have been so kind to me with all your presents. Allow me to present you with some clothes."

And he gave the miller's son the most beautiful clothes made out of satin and gold thread. The miller's son looked so handsome, the King's daughter fell in love with him right away.

Meanwhile, Puss had raced ahead to where some farmers were working in a field.

"If the King stops and asks you who owns this land, you must say that it belongs to the Marquis of Carabas. If you don't do this, bad things will happen to you."

The farmers were so scared that they agreed at once. Then Puss ran up to some harvesters who were cutting corn, and told them to do exactly the same thing. The harvesters were so scared that they, too, agreed.

When the King's carriage stopped at the field where the farmers were working, the King leaned out and asked, "To whom does this land belong?"

The farmers replied, "The Marquis of Carabas, sire." A little further up the road, the King's carriage stopped again opposite the harvesters.

"Who owns these fields?" asked the King. "Why, the Marquis of Carabas, sire," said the harvesters.

"This Marquis of Carabas must be a very rich man," thought the King.

While all this was happening, Puss in Boots had run ahead to a large castle where a magician lived. The magician was the real owner of the land that the King had been driving through.

"I hear that you can change yourself into anything you choose," said Puss to the magician.

"Well, almost anything," said the magician, proudly.

"How about a lion?" asked Puss.

"Oh, that's easy," said the magician, and instantly turned himself into a big, roaring lion. Even Puss was frightened, and had to hide behind a chair.

When the magician had turned back into a man, Puss said, "That was very scary! But lions are big. Could you change yourself into something small, like a mouse?"

"Of course!" laughed the magician, and instantly turned himself into a tiny mouse and scurried across the floor. That was a mistake. Clever old Puss chased him, caught him and ate him all up.

Just then, Puss heard the King's carriage rattling along the road to the castle. He ran outside to meet it.

"Welcome to the home of my master, the Marquis of Carabas," said Puss, as the carriage reached the front door. The King looked around at the huge castle and realised that he would find no better husband for his daughter.

"I know that my daughter already loves you," he told the miller's son. "Would you do me the great service of agreeing to marry her?"

The miller's son had already fallen in love with the King's daughter, so agreed to the marriage at once.

The happy couple were married shortly after, and Puss lived in great comfort for the rest of his days.

Little Red Riding Hood

nce upon a time there was a nice little girl who lived with her mother in a nice little cottage at the edge of a deep, dark forest. The girl was known as Little Red Riding Hood because she always wore a beautiful red cape with a hood.

One day, her mother called to her from the kitchen. "Little Red Riding Hood, Granny is not feeling very well. Will you take her some goodies I've packed for her?"
"Of course I will," said Little Red Riding Hood, who loved her Granny very much.

She ran downstairs and peeked into the basket her mother had packed. It was full of delicious things. There were homemade cookies, a jam tart, some cherry muffins and, to finish it all off, the biggest, reddest apple that Little Red Riding Hood had ever seen.

Granny's cottage lay on the other side of the forest. "Now, remember," said Little Red Riding Hood's mother, "keep to the path and don't talk to any strangers."
"I won't," replied Little Red Riding Hood and, picking up the basket, she skipped merrily out the door.

It was a lovely day and Little Red Riding Hood sang a merry tune to herself as she made her way along the path.

A little while later, when she was in the deepest, darkest part of the forest, she saw some pretty flowers growing in a small clearing just off the path. "I'm sure Mother wouldn't mind if I went off the path for a minute to pick some flowers. Granny would love them," she thought. She had a quick look around, didn't see anyone, so ran to the little clearing, where she started to pick the flowers.

But, hiding behind a tree, was a not-very-nice wolf, who was hungry and looking for his dinner. In one swift movement, he was at Little Red Riding Hood's side.

"Hello, my dear," he said, in his most charming voice. "What a beautiful day! I see you're picking flowers. May I help you?"

Little Red Riding Hood was startled to see the wolf at first, but he seemed so friendly and had such a lovely deep voice, her fears faded away. "I'm picking them for my Granny. She's not very well. I'm taking her this basket of food."

"What a lovely thing to do!" exclaimed the wolf, thinking that if he was clever, he might be able to eat the girl, her Granny and the basket of food for his dinner.

"I've got an idea," said the wolf. "Why don't I run ahead and give the basket to your Granny, while you finish picking your pretty flowers. Then we can all meet at her house. Hmm?"

"That's a very good idea," said Little Red Hiding Hood. "She lives a little further up the path in the first cottage."

"That's settled, then," said the wolf, taking the basket from her. "By the way, what's your name?"

"Little Red Riding Hood," she answered.

"Charmed to meet you, my dear," said the wolf, with a big, wide grin. "See you soon."

And he set off down the path towards Granny's cottage, licking his lips.

When he arrived at Granny's cottage, he knocked on the door.
"Hello! Is there anyone at home?" shouted the wolf in his best little girl's voice.
"Who's there?" asked Granny, tucked up in bed.
"It's me, Granny," said the wolf, "Little Red Riding Hood."
"Come in, dear," said Granny. "I'm in bed."

The wolf opened the door and ran upstairs, into Granny's bedroom.
"You're not Little Red Riding Hood!" exclaimed Granny.
"You're absolutely right!" said the wolf, and before she had a chance to say anything else, he leapt over to her bedside, opened his mouth as wide as he could, and gobbled Granny right up.
"And now for Little Red Riding Hood," thought the wolf. He put on Granny's shawl, nightcap and glasses as fast as he could, and dived into the bed.
"What a clever wolf I am," he chuckled to himself.

A short time later, Little Red Riding Hood arrived at Granny's cottage and knocked on the door.

"Who's there?" asked the wolf in his best Granny voice.

"It's me, Granny. Little Red Riding Hood," said Little Red Riding Hood.

"Let yourself in, dear," said the wolf.

Little Red Riding Hood opened the door and went into Granny's bedroom.

"What big eyes you have," said Little Red Riding Hood.

"All the better to see you with, my dear," replied the wolf.

"What big ears you have," said Little Red Riding Hood.

"All the better to hear you with, my dear," replied the wolf.

"And what big teeth you have," said Little Red Riding Hood.

"All the better to EAT you with!" said the wolf, and leaped out of bed and gobbled her up in an instant. Still feeling hungry, the wolf also ate all the food in the basket. Then he gave a huge burp.

But, a woodcutter working nearby had heard all the noise coming from Granny's cottage. He burst through the door and, when he saw the wolf, killed him with one mighty blow of his axe. Then he slit open the wolf's tummy and Little Red Riding Hood and her Granny popped out, alive and well. They were so relieved to be rescued, they hugged each other tightly.

"Thank you!" said Granny to the woodcutter.

"I'm only happy that you and Little Red Riding Hood are safe," he replied.

"I hope this teaches you never to talk to strangers again," said Granny to Little Red Riding Hood.

Little Red Riding Hood promised that she wouldn't, and she never did, however charming and helpful they seemed to be.

Three Billy Goats Gruff

any years ago there were three billy goats that lived in the hills. There was a small billy goat, a medium-sized billy goat and a big billy goat. They all shared the same name: Gruff.

These goats didn't do very much. They sometimes liked to play hide-and-seek with each other, which was a good game to play with so many rocks to hide behind! But, usually they just ate and slept.

Unfortunately, eating was becoming a problem. Over the years, the Three Billy Goats Gruff were finding that good, sweet, eating grass was becoming harder and harder to find. They had to look longer each day for the thin tufts of grass that grew between the rocks. Things were getting so bad that the Three Billy Goats Gruff were feeling hungry all the time, and their tummies were getting smaller and smaller.

"We haven't had a good meal in ages," moaned the middle-sized billy goat. "My tummy's so empty it's making growling noises."
"We can't go on like this," said the biggest billy goat.
"I know where there's enough sweet, green grass to keep us full for the rest of our lives," said the small billy goat.
The other goats' ears pricked up at once.
"Where?" they demanded.
"In the big field that lies across the river," replied the small billy goat, proudly.

"But we can't get across the river," the two bigger goats groaned.
"Oh, yes, we can," said the small goat brightly. "There's a bridge that
crosses the river."

The two bigger goats explained patiently to the small goat that there was a horrible troll who lived under the bridge. If anyone tried to cross it, the troll leaped out from under the bridge and killed them where they stood. "That's why there's so much grass on the other side. No one dares to cross the bridge!" said the middle-sized billy goat.

"Hmm . . . let me think about this," said the small billy goat, who was the cleverest of the three, and wandered off to have a little think.

Some time later, the small goat went back to the other two goats, who were having a little nap under the shade of a large rock. He told them that he'd thought of a way they could cross the bridge without being eaten by the troll. The two bigger goats listened to his plan and then agreed that with no food left on their side of the bridge, they'd have to give his plan a try.

Later that evening, when the Three Billy Goats Gruff searched around the rocks for something to eat, they couldn't find even one blade of grass. They finally gave up and settled down to sleep, their stomachs rumbling with hunger.

Early the next morning, the goats woke up, stretched their legs, gingerly made their way down to the riverbank and walked towards the bridge. "I'm scared," said the middle-sized goat. "What if the troll eats us all up?" "We must keep to the plan," said the small goat. "If we keep to the plan, everything will be all right." "We must cross the bridge and get to the field. We'll starve to death if we don't," said the biggest goat. "If only we could swim," moaned the middle-sized goat. "Then we wouldn't have to bother with the bridge at all!"

When they arrived at the bridge, the small billy goat started nervously across.

"Good luck!" shouted the other two goats, who were waiting on the bank.

As he got towards the middle of the bridge, all was quiet.

"Maybe the troll's gone away," thought the small goat, hopefully.

Suddenly, the troll leaped out from under the bridge and stood right in his way.

"And what do you think you're doing?" asked the troll, glowering at him.

"Just trying to cross the b . . . b . . . bridge, sir," the small goat stuttered back in a tiny voice.

"How dare you try to cross my bridge!" the troll yelled at him. "I think I'll eat you for my dinner."

"Oh, I wouldn't do that, sir," said the small goat. "Look how skinny I am. I wouldn't make a good meal at all. But I have a friend who will be passing by in a while. He's much bigger than me. He'd make a much better meal."

The troll thought about this.

"Hmm . . . all right, you may pass."

He stepped aside and allowed the small goat to reach the other side safely.

Then the middle-sized goat tried to cross the bridge. As soon as he got to the middle, the troll leaped out from under it and barred his way.

"And what do you think you're doing?" asked the troll, glowering at him.

"Just trying to cross the b . . . b . . . bridge, sir," the middle-sized goat stuttered back in a small voice.

"How dare you try to cross my bridge!" the troll yelled at him. "I think I'll eat you for my dinner."

"Oh, I wouldn't do that, sir," said the middle-sized goat. "Look how skinny I am. I wouldn't make a good meal at all. But, I have a friend who will be passing by in a while. He's much bigger than me. He'd make a much better meal."

Again the troll thought about this.
"Hmm . . . all right, you may pass."
The troll stepped aside and allowed the middle-sized goat to reach the other side safely.

Then it was the biggest goat's turn. As soon as he reached the middle of the bridge, the troll once more leaped out from under it.

"And what do you think you're doing?" asked the troll, glowering at the biggest goat.

"I'm trying to cross the bridge," replied the biggest goat, quite calmly. "And you're in my way."

"How dare you speak to me like that," said the troll, turning red with anger. "You'll pay for that! I'm going to kill you and eat you for my dinner."

But, before he had a chance to say or do anything else, the biggest goat lowered his huge horns, ran up to the troll and, with one flick of his head, tossed the troll over the bridge and into the river.

The unfortunate troll disappeared beneath the water and was never seen or heard of again.

When the biggest goat joined his friends on the other side, they all leaped around and kicked the air in excitement.

"We've done it!" they cried. "We've done it!"

Then they began to eat the sweet, fresh, beautiful, green grass that lay all around them. They ate and ate until their tummies were full. Then they fell into a long peaceful sleep under the shade of a large tree. And the Three Billy Goats Gruff, never, ever went hungry again.

Three Little Pigs

 nce upon a time there was an old sow who had three little piglets. When they were old enough, she told them that they should leave home and make their own way in the world. The first little pig met a man carrying a large bundle of straw. The pig thought that a house made of straw would make a very fine house indeed. So he bought the straw from the man and, in no time at all, had built himself a house. The house looked very nice, but wasn't very strong.

One day, a hungry wolf came passing by and saw the pig sitting in his house, enjoying a cup of tea.

"What a nice pig," he thought. "He would fill me up."

So he went and knocked on the door. "Little pig, little pig, let me come in," said the wolf.

"Not by the hair of my chinny chin chin!" said the frightened pig.

"Then I'll huff, and I'll puff, and I'll blow your house down!" cried the wolf.

Then he huffed, and he puffed, and he blew down the little pig's house of straw. Instantly, the wolf was at the pig's side and he gobbled him up.

Meanwhile, the second little pig had met a man who was carrying a large pile of sticks.
"Those are just the sort of sticks I need to build myself a house," thought the pig.
He bought the sticks and, after working very hard, had soon built himself a house. The house looked very nice, but wasn't very strong.

Not long after, the wolf passed by and noticed the pig sitting at his window, enjoying a slice of cake.

"Another pig!" he thought. "I'm in luck!"

He went and knocked on the front door.

"Little pig, little pig, let me come in," said the wolf.

"Not by the hair of my chinny chin chin!" said the frightened pig.

"Then I'll huff, and I'll puff, and I'll blow your house down!" cried the wolf.

Then he huffed, and he puffed, and he blew down the little pig's house of sticks.

In one bound, the wolf was at the pig's side and he ate him all up.

"Two pigs in one week," thought the wolf, licking his lips. "Life can't get much better than this!"

The third little pig had also met a man, and that man was carrying a large load of bricks.

"These bricks would make a strong house for me to live in," thought the pig. So he bought the bricks, and soon had built himself a house. The house looked very nice, and was very strong.

One day, the wolf passed by and saw the pig eating an apple pie.
"Another pig," thought the wolf. "Hooray!"
He went and knocked on the door. "Little pig, little pig, let me come in."
"Not by the hair of my chinny chin chin!" said the pig, who was not at
all frightened and just carried on eating his apple pie.
"Then I'll huff, and I'll puff, and I'll blow your house down!" cried
the wolf.
Well, the wolf huffed, and he puffed, and tried to blow the house down
but, it was so strong, it didn't move at all. The wolf tried harder and
huffed and puffed with all his might, but the house still wouldn't
fall down.
The wolf decided to try to trick the pig out of his house.

"Oh, little piggy," the wolf shouted through the door. "There are some lovely turnips growing in the field next door. Why don't you and I get up bright and early tomorrow morning and go pick some?"

"What a good idea," said the pig. "See you here at seven o'clock."

But the clever pig got to the field at six o'clock and picked all the turnips he needed. By the time the wolf arrived at seven o'clock, the pig was safely back in his house again.

The wolf was very angry that the pig had fooled him, but he had another trick up his sleeve.

"Oh, little piggy," he shouted. "There are some juicy ripe apples just waiting to be picked in the orchard down the road. Why don't we meet there this afternoon and pick some together?"

"What a good idea," said the pig. "See you there after lunch."

But when the wolf arrived at the orchard, the little pig was already up an apple tree. When he saw the wolf, the pig threw an apple as far as he could. While the wolf chased after it, the pig quickly climbed down the tree, got into a barrel and rolled all the way home.

When the wolf realized that the pig had tricked him again, he was furious. He was so angry, he walked all the way back to the pig's house and climbed onto the roof. He decided to climb down the chimney to catch the pig. But the clever pig had placed a large pot of boiling water in his fireplace. The wolf came down the chimney and fell straight into the pot of boiling water! The pig quickly put on the lid, and that evening sat down to a lovely meal of boiled wolf with turnips from the field next door. He finished his meal off with a big, juicy apple from the orchard down the road. What a very clever pig he was.

Cinderella

There once lived a man who had a kind and pretty wife and a beautiful daughter. Sadly, the man's wife died soon after their daughter was born. A few years later, the man decided to marry again. His second wife was not kind and pretty, and she already had two daughters who were even less kind and pretty than she was. In fact, her daughters were so selfish, proud and greedy that they were known as the "ugly sisters".

From the first day they moved in, the ugly sisters were cruel and unkind to their stepsister. They spent all day doing nothing but gossiping and buying new dresses and trying to make themselves look pretty. Meanwhile, they made their poor stepsister do all the housework. She had to clean the house from top to bottom, do all the cooking, wash and scour the pots and pans and clear out the cinders from the fireplace. She spent so much time doing this that her stepsisters called her "Cinderella". Soon, poor Cinderella was tired out from working so hard. She began to look pale and thin, and her one dress started to look ragged and dirty.

One day, the King and Queen decided to hold a grand ball. Everyone in the town was hoping for an invitation, especially the two ugly sisters who each secretly thought that they might be able to marry the Prince. They couldn't believe their luck when, the very next day, an invitation arrived. That afternoon, they went on a huge shopping trip and came back with bags full of dresses, shoes and make-up. For the next few days, all they did was try on their new clothes. They couldn't decide what to wear for the ball.

When the big night arrived, the ugly sisters were still unsure what to wear, so they paraded their new clothes in front of poor Cinderella and asked her to tell them what suited them best.
"What a pity you're not invited to the ball, Cinders," one of them smirked to Cinderella.
"She's got nothing to wear," giggled the other one. "She couldn't possibly come in that old rag."
"Poor Cinderella," said the first one. "Never mind. We'll tell you all about it when we come back."
And with those words, they both swept out of the door and into their waiting carriage.
"Bye . . . Cinders," they both waved, leaning out of the carriage door.
"Make sure the house is clean and neat for our return."
The carriage sped off into the night, whisking the excited ugly sisters to the ball, leaving poor Cinderella all alone.

After they'd left, Cinderella sat on the little stool near the fire.
"Why are my sisters so cruel to me?" she thought. "I do everything they tell me to do around the house, and more! They never thank me for it, or give me a kind word, or even smile at me." She felt so unhappy she began to cry. She would have loved one night of happiness at the ball.

Suddenly, a beautiful woman, carrying a silver wand, appeared right in front of her. She seemed to have come from nowhere.

"Who are you?" gasped Cinderella, a little frightened.

"Don't be scared. I am your Fairy Godmother," said the beautiful woman. "What's the matter, child? Why are you crying?"

"I would have loved to have gone to the ball," wept Cinderella. "But my stepsisters don't want me to go. Even if they did, I have nothing to wear and no carriage to take me there."

"Don't worry," said her Fairy Godmother, kindly. "This is your special day, Cinderella. You shall go to the ball! But, first, I'd like you to bring me some things. I need a pumpkin, two mice and the biggest rat you can find."

Cinderella rushed around the house and looked in all the mouse and rat traps. Soon there was a pumpkin, along with two little white mice in a box and a large rat, scurrying around in its cage, all lying at the Fairy Godmother's feet. With one wave of her silver wand, the Fairy Godmother changed the pumpkin into a golden coach, the mice into two magnificent white horses and the rat into a coachman.

Cinderella was astonished, and then looked down at her terrible dress. "But I can't go to the ball in this," she cried.

With another wave of her wand, the Fairy Godmother changed Cinderella's ragged dress into a ball gown made of the finest satin and silver thread. On her feet were a pair of beautiful glass slippers.

"Now, go and enjoy yourself," said the Fairy Godmother. "But be sure to be back before midnight, for when the clock strikes twelve everything will return to what it was before."

Cinderella stepped into the glistening carriage and was whisked through the dark streets until she reached the palace.

When she entered the ballroom, everyone stopped what they were doing and stared. They had never seen such a beautiful girl before. The Prince fell in love with her as soon as he saw her, and danced with her all evening. Cinderella thought that he was the most handsome man she had ever seen and fell in love with him, too. Cinderella was having such a wonderful time, she forgot all about her Fairy Godmother's warning. All of a sudden, she heard the clock strike twelve.

"Oh, no," she thought, "I must leave!"
She tore herself from the Prince's arms and rushed out of the ballroom.
Before she reached the palace gates at the end of the drive, her beautiful
dress had already turned back into the shabby, dirty dress that she
always wore.

Back in the ballroom, the Prince couldn't understand why this lovely
girl had suddenly run away. He searched the Palace for her, but couldn't
find her anywhere. But, in her rush to leave, Cinderella had left behind
one of her glass slippers. When the Prince found it on the Palace steps,
he immediately issued a proclamation, saying that he intended to find
and marry the girl whose foot fitted the glass slipper. He would visit
every house in the land, until he had found her.

The ugly sisters became very excited. On the day that the Prince was going to visit their house, they made sure to wear their best dresses.

When the Prince arrived, he held out the glass slipper and asked which one of the sisters would like to try it on first.

"I will!" cried one of them. But, as much as she tried to push and, squeeze her foot into the slipper, it just wouldn't fit. Her foot was far too big.

"Give it to me!" said the other sister and, grabbing the slipper, tried to put it on. But her foot was far too big, too. However much she pushed and tugged, she just couldn't get her foot into it.

Just then, Cinderella stepped forward. She had been standing quietly in the shadows and no one had noticed her.

"May I try?" she asked, shyly.

"You!" cried the ugly sisters. "Of course you can't! Now get back to the kitchen where you belong!"

"Be quiet!" ordered the Prince. "Of course you may," he said, turning to Cinderella, not recognizing her. Cinderella sat down and put the slipper onto her foot. There was no pushing or pulling. It glided on perfectly. The ugly sisters gasped in amazement.

"I recognize you now," said the Prince, smiling. "You are the girl I fell in love with at the ball, and you are the girl I am going to marry."

"I can't believe this is happening," cried Cinderella. "I loved you the moment I met you, and I thought I'd never see you again."

Cinderella and the prince had a glorious wedding. She forgave her sisters their cruelty, and she never had to wash up a dirty dish ever again.

The Princess and The Frog

Long, long ago, there was a King who had three lovely daughters who all lived together in a magnificent castle. The King's youngest daughter liked the simple things in life. She enjoyed walking in the castle grounds, humming songs to herself. She loved the sweet scent of the flowers and watching all the little animals scurrying around the woods.

One day, the Princess found herself at the furthest point of the castle grounds. Here stood an old well that had not been used for many years. The Princess sat on the edge of the well and started to throw a small golden ball in the air. She caught it and threw it up again, this time a little higher. The next time she caught it, she threw it higher still. But the next time, the ball went so high she couldn't catch it at all, and it fell all the way down into the murky waters of the well.

"I've had that ball ever since I was a baby," thought the Princess. She was so upset at losing her precious golden ball, she began to cry.

"I'll get it back for you," she heard a voice say.

The Princess stopped crying and looked around but couldn't see anyone.

"I wonder where that voice came from," she thought.

"I'm here," said the voice.

The Princess looked down and saw that the voice belonged to a frog that was staring up at her.

"But you're a frog!" exclaimed the astonished Princess.

"I am a frog," replied the frog. "And I will get your ball back on the condition that you look after me. You must take me back to the castle with you and treat me as you would treat your best friend. You must play with me, allow me to eat from your plate at the table and let me sleep in your bed. If you agree to all this, I will bring your ball back."

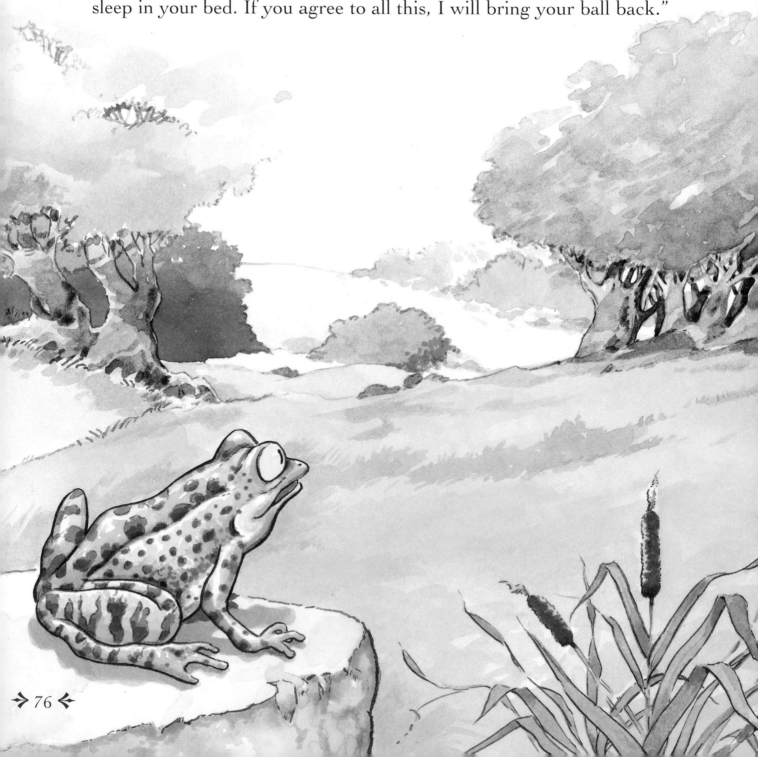

Although the Princess loved animals, she hated the idea of spending so much time with a slimy frog. But she wanted her golden ball back so much that she agreed to his conditions at once. The frog dived into the well and, shortly after, reappeared with the ball in his mouth. The Princess did not want to take the frog back home with her, so she took the ball from him and ran back to the castle as fast as she could, leaving the poor frog at the well.

That evening, the Princess and her sisters were sitting with their father having their dinner when she heard a strange noise. It was a funny flip-flop sound and it appeared to be coming up the stairs to the dining room. Then she heard a little scratching noise at the door.

"I wonder what that is," she thought, getting off her chair. She opened the door but there was no one there. Then she heard a little croak at her feet. She looked down and saw the frog staring up at her with his big round eyes.

"Oh, no!" thought the Princess. "He's found me!"

"Hello, Princess," said the frog. "That wasn't very nice, running away from me like that. Here I am to make sure you keep your promise to look after me."

Then the frog hopped across the room and, with one big leap, landed on the edge of the table.

"What is the meaning of all this?" asked the King, a little harshly.

"I lost my ball down the well," began the Princess. "This frog got it back for me and, in return, I promised to look after him. But I don't want to!"

"I see," said the King, stroking his beard, thoughtfully. "I'm sorry, my dear," he finally said to the Princess. "But a promise is a promise. And a promise must be kept. I'm afraid that you must look after our little friend for as long as he wishes."

"Very well, father," answered the Princess meekly and sat back down at the table.

With one hop, the frog was at her side.

"Mmmm, that looks delicious," said the frog, looking at the food on the Princess's plate. "Feed me some of that, please."

The Princess really didn't like the thought of having to put her fingers anywhere near the frog, but obediently popped a morsel of food into his waiting mouth.

"Yuck," she thought.

"That was very tasty. More, please!" said the frog.

So the poor Princess had to feed the frog all evening, and found it so disgusting that she completely lost her appetite.

At the end of dinner, the Princess got down from her chair and walked angrily across the room towards the stairs.

"That was the worst meal, ever!" she muttered under her breath. "I hate looking after that frog!"

She opened the big door and stomped up the stairs to her bedroom.

"I'm a bit tired, too," yawned the frog who, after bidding good night to the King and the Princess's sisters, hopped across the room and followed the Princess up the stairs.

In her bedroom, the Princess quickly got into her nightgown, brushed her teeth and jumped into bed. Out of the corner of her eye, she'd noticed that the frog had come into the room and was crouching quietly in the corner.

"And you can sleep right where you are!" she yelled at him. "I don't want your ugly body anywhere near me!"

"You know, there is one way you can be rid of me," said the frog, jumping into bed beside her. "If you were to give me one kiss on my lips I would leave here immediately and never return."

"That's the most horrible thing I've ever heard of!" cried the Princess.

"Your lips are so slimy!"

"Well, it's up to you," said the frog. "But remember, you'd never see me again."

The more she thought about it, the more the Princess realized that if she wanted to be rid of the frog, she'd just have to overcome her disgust and kiss his green, slippery mouth.

She pursed her lips, shut her eyes and kissed the frog's lips as quickly as she could.

All at once, there was a sudden blinding flash and to the Princess's utter astonishment the frog had completely disappeared and in its place stood a young, handsome Prince.

The Prince explained that a wicked witch had cast a spell on him many years before that had turned him into a frog and the only person who could break the spell would be a young, lovely Princess who would kiss him on the lips. The Prince and Princess liked each other very much and talked far into the night until they both fell asleep. In the morning, they both shyly agreed that they would like to get married.

The King was overjoyed that his youngest daughter had fallen in love, and was happy to give his consent to the marriage. After the wedding, the Prince took his new bride to live in his own land. Everyone at his castle welcomed him home, happy to see the return of their Prince whom they'd thought was lost to them forever.

The Ugly Duckling

t was summer in the country. Everyone felt hot and lazy in the strong sun. In the moat that surrounded the old castle, a mother duck had laid her eggs among the rushes. She had sat for a long time waiting for her brood to hatch. Finally, one by one, the eggs began to crack and she heard the first "quack, quack" of her new ducklings.

Soon, all the eggs had hatched except for one. This was the largest egg of all and it was becoming very difficult for the mother duck to sit comfortably on it.

"Are you all right?" asked a friendly duck, who happened to swim by.

"I'm fine, thank you," replied the mother duck. "It's just that my last egg here is taking a long time to hatch. As you can see, it's quite big to get comfortable on, especially in this heat."

"Yes, you do look tired," said the friendly duck. "I'm sure it will hatch soon."

Just then, both ducks heard a tiny scraping sound and then a cracking sound as the egg began to break. Suddenly, out popped the last duckling. It was the strangest, ugliest-looking duckling either of them had ever seen.

"Oh, dear," said the friendly duck. "What an odd shape he is. He must have been in the shell too long."

"Never mind," said the mother duck. "I'm sure he'll look just like my other ducklings in a few weeks. Anyway, he's my son and I love him whatever he looks like."
"Of course," grinned the friendly duck and, with a "see you later!" paddled gently away.

"Come on, everyone," said the mother duck to her new ducklings. "Let's get you swimming." All the ducklings lined up behind their mother and, with their little legs paddling furiously, swam towards the middle of the moat.

"Here's mother duck with her new ducklings," all the other ducks cried, when they saw the little procession.

"But look at that one on the end," said one, pointing to the ugly duckling.

"That's the ugliest duckling I've ever seen!" said another.

It seemed that all the ducks in the moat were laughing at the ugly duckling.

As the weeks went by, the ugly duckling's brothers and sisters grew
bigger and stronger. They looked more and more like proper ducks with
each passing day. But the ugly duckling seemed to grow even stranger-
looking, with his dull, grey feathers and peculiar shape. Because he
looked different, the other young ducklings laughed at him, and didn't
want him to play with them. The ugly duckling felt so sad and lonely he
began to hide among the tall rushes where no one would see him.

Once, he saw three beautiful, white birds flying overhead. They seemed so happy and free. In some strange way he felt he was related to these lovely birds in the sky.

"But how could I be?" he thought. "They are so beautiful and I am so ugly." And so he stayed in his hiding place among the reeds where no one would see him.

When winter came, the waters of the moat froze over and the ugly duckling was stuck fast in the ice. He couldn't move at all, not even to get food. As the days went by, the ice showed no sign of melting and it seemed that the ugly duckling might starve to death.

One day, a man passed by and noticed the poor duckling stuck in the ice. The man was kind and he brought his axe to free the duckling. Tenderly, he lifted the ugly duckling from the frozen waters and took him home.

The man cared for the ugly duckling as if he was his own child, keeping him warm and making sure he had enough to eat. But, as comfortable as life was in the man's house, the ugly duckling knew that he did not really belong there. So, when the waters of the moat thawed out, he went back to his hiding place in the reeds once more.

Soon, the flowers began to bloom and the days became warmer. It was spring again. To his surprise, the ugly duckling noticed that his wings had grown much larger than those of the other ducklings. One day he started to flap them. He rose out from the reeds and began to fly. He enjoyed the feeling of flying free through the air, and flew for a long time, until he came to a large lake. Looking down, he saw three lovely, white birds swimming in the water. They looked just like the ones he had seen flying overhead months before. The ugly duckling flew down to get a closer look. As he neared the surface of the lake, he saw a reflection of another of the lovely birds. The ugly duckling looked around, but there were no other birds in the sky.

Then he realised that he was looking at his own reflection in the water! He was the lovely bird flying so gracefully in the sky. He wasn't an ugly duckling after all. He was a beautiful, white swan.

The other swans all swam up to greet their new friend. The young swan was shy at first, not being used to all the attention. And he was just getting used to the idea that he wasn't a plain, ugly duckling. But the other swans were so kind and gentle, he soon felt completely at home with them. He couldn't believe his good fortune, and was overjoyed that he had finally found the place where he belonged.

Snow White

ne winter's day, a Queen sat at a window, sewing. Suddenly, she pricked her finger and a drop of blood fell onto the snow below. She liked the bright red of the blood against the whiteness of the snow. She hoped that one day she would give birth to a child with lovely, snow-white skin and bright, blood-red lips.

The very next year, the Queen gave birth to a baby daughter. The baby had the whitest of skin and the reddest of lips. The Queen called her child Snow White and she loved her daughter dearly. Sadly, the Queen died the very same year.

After some time, Snow White's father, the King, married again. His new Queen was very beautiful but she was also vain and proud. She owned a special mirror, and every morning she asked the mirror the same question.

"Mirror, mirror, on the wall, who is the fairest of them all?"

"You are, O Queen," the mirror would also reply.

And every morning the Queen would smile to herself, for she knew that the mirror always told the truth.

As the years passed, Snow White was slowly turning into a beautiful young woman. One morning, the Queen awoke and asked the mirror her usual question.

"Mirror, mirror, on the wall, who is the fairest of them all?"

But this time, the mirror replied:

"You, O Queen, are fair, it's true, but Snow White is now fairer than you."

The Queen turned green with envy. No one was allowed to be more beautiful than her. Even though Snow White was dearly loved by the King, the twisted, jealous Queen decided to have her killed as soon as possible. She summoned the royal huntsman and told him to take Snow White into the forest and kill her. She told him to cut out Snow White's heart and bring it to her, to prove that she was dead.

The huntsman took Snow White into the forest, but, as he was about to kill her, looked at her frightened face. He felt so sorry for her, he told her to run away and hide deeper in the forest. Then he killed a wild boar and cut out its heart so he could pretend that it was Snow White's heart, when he showed it to the Queen.

Snow White ran further and further into the forest. When she could run no more, she stopped and leaned against a tree to get her breath back. Out of the corner of her eye she noticed a small cottage, half hidden by the trees. She went up to the cottage and knocked on the door. There was no reply. She opened the door and went in.

In front of her was a little table with seven little cups and seven little plates on it. There was food on the plates and water in the cups. The cottage belonged to seven dwarfs who worked all day in a silver mine. Snow White was very hungry and thirsty, so she took a little bit of food from each plate, and a little bit of water from each cup. She was a very thoughtful girl and didn't want to empty one person's plate and cup completely. After she'd eaten, she felt very tired. She went upstairs and found a room with seven beds in it. She lay down on one of the beds and fell fast asleep.

When the seven dwarfs returned home, they each found a little bit of food missing from their plates and a little bit of water missing from their cups. When they went upstairs, they found something even stranger. There was a beautiful young girl sleeping in one of their beds! They woke her and asked her what she was doing there. Snow White burst into tears and, after she'd stopped crying, told them her terrible story. The seven dwarfs felt so sorry for her, they invited her to stay with them.

"But I can't pay you anything for my food and bed," Snow White cried. "I have no money."

The dwarfs told her, that as long as she cooked and kept the cottage clean for them, she was welcome to stay as long as she liked.

"Thank you so much. I'll do my best to look after you," said Snow White, happily.

Back at the castle, the wicked Queen took what she thought was Snow White's heart and had great pleasure feeding it to the dogs. The next morning, she stood in front of her mirror.

"Mirror, mirror, on the wall, who is the fairest of them all?"

"You, O Queen, are fair, it's true, but Snow White is still fairer than you," the mirror replied.

The Queen screamed in anger. She knew that the mirror never lied, so Snow White must still be alive. She found out where Snow White was living and decided to play a horrible trick on her. The Queen disguised herself as a peddler selling little trinkets, pieces of lace and pretty brooches, and went to the dwarfs' cottage and knocked on the door.

"Hello, my dear," croaked the Queen, pretending to be the peddler. "I've got some lovely little things here you may care to see."

"Oh, isn't it lovely!" Snow White exclaimed, as the Queen held up a pretty bow.

The Queen convinced Snow White that she needed a new length of braid for her bodice but, when she helped Snow White put it on, she pulled it so tightly that all the breath went out of Snow White's body. The Queen left her, believing she was dead.

When the seven dwarfs arrived home from work that evening, they were shocked to find Snow White lying on the floor. She didn't seem to be breathing. When they saw how tightly her bodice was tied, they quickly cut it loose. The dwarfs were relieved and delighted when she started to breathe again. They made her promise them that she'd never accept anything from a stranger in future.

Meanwhile, the Queen rushed back to the palace, ripped off her disguise and stood in front of her mirror.

"Mirror, mirror, on the wall, who is the fairest of them all?" she asked.
"You, O Queen, are fair, it's true, but Snow White is still fairer than
you," the mirror replied.
The Queen was speechless with rage when she realised that Snow
White was still alive.
"I'll think of another way to trick her," she thought. "And this time,
death will not escape her!"

The Queen picked an apple that had one red side and one yellow side.
She then injected a deadly poison into the red side and disguised herself
once more: this time as an old peasant woman. She went to the dwarfs'
cottage and knocked on the door again. Snow White went to answer the
knock, and was a little wary at first, but the old peasant woman was so
nice and friendly, she quickly relaxed and they were soon chatting away.

After they had been talking for some time, the disguised Queen offered
Snow White the poisoned apple.

"That's very kind of you," said Snow White. "But I'm not supposed to
take anything from strangers."

"Don't worry. There's nothing wrong with this apple," said the Queen.
"And to prove it to you, I'll take a bite out of it first."

With a great crunch, the Queen took a large bite out of the yellow side
of the apple. Then she offered the poisoned, red side to Snow White.

"I suppose it's all right, and it does look delicious," said Snow White.
As soon as she had taken a bite out of the apple, the poor girl fell dead
at the Queen's feet. The Queen rushed back to the palace and ripped off
her disguise.

"Mirror, mirror, on the wall, who is the fairest of them all?" she asked the mirror.

"You are, O Queen," it replied.

The Queen shrieked with joy. She had succeeded. Snow White was well and truly dead.

When the dwarfs arrived home that evening, they could not wake Snow White. They stayed with her all night, hoping that she might wake up, but in the morning they realized that she must be dead. With heavy hearts, they put her on a bed and, with bowed heads, stood guard over her. Snow White remained beautiful, even in death.

Years passed, and news of Snow White's beauty had spread far and wide. One day, a Prince decided to see the beautiful girl for himself. Her beauty took his breath away and he fell in love with her instantly. Tenderly, the Prince lifted Snow White's head to kiss her. But as he did so, the tiny piece of apple that had poisoned her, fell from her lips. Gradually, she began to stir.

"What has happened?" she asked drowsily.

The seven dwarfs jumped up and down with joy that she was alive.

When Snow White's father, the King, heard of the terrible things the Queen had done to his daughter, he banished her from his land forever. Before long, Snow White and her Prince were married. But she never forgot the kindness the seven dwarfs had shown her for the rest of her life.

The Princess and The Pea

In a distant land, there lived a Prince who decided one day, that he wanted nothing more in the world than to marry a beautiful Princess. His parents, the King and Queen, agreed that he was now old enough to marry and wished him well in his hunt.

For the next two years he journeyed far and wide to find his perfect wife. But the Prince was a very choosy person and, although he met lots of Princesses along the way, he always found something wrong with them. They were either too short or too tall. Too fat or too thin. Too happy or too sad, or just too nice!

When he returned home, he was very upset that he couldn't find the right Princess to marry.

"There, there," said the Queen, comforting her son. "I know it must be terribly upsetting for you, dear, but I'm sure that the right Princess will come along one day."

"But I might be an old man by the time that happens," moaned the unfortunate Prince.

"Now," said his father, the King, "things aren't that bad. You're still young, rich, handsome and a Prince! You're bound to find the right girl soon."

"But, when?" cried the Prince.

In truth, the King and Queen were a bit fed up with their son (who was acting a bit spoiled) and decided to send him away to one of their other castles for a complete rest.

One night, there was a terrible storm. Thunder and lightening filled the sky. The windows rattled and the wind whistled around the rooms of the old castle.

As the storm raged on, there was a knock on the huge castle door. The Queen opened it and standing before her was a young girl who was shivering from the cold and the rain.

"My goodness," said the Queen. "What a dreadful night to be outside. You're soaked through, my dear. You'd better come in and we'll find you some dry clothes."

"How kind of you," said the girl.

The Queen led her to the drawing room where she could dry herself by the large, crackling fire.

"Do you live nearby?" asked the Queen.

"No, Your Majesty," replied the girl. "I'm a Princess from another land. My carriage is stuck in the mud, a little way down the road."

As the Queen and the girl talked, the Queen began to realize that this young Princess might make the perfect wife for her son. She wasn't too short or too tall. She wasn't too fat or too thin. She wasn't too happy or too sad and, although she seemed very nice, she didn't seem to be too nice. But the Queen wanted to make sure the girl was a real Princess so that they wouldn't be disappointed. She had an idea how she could find out.

"My dear," said the Queen. "We can't possibly let you leave on such a terrible night as this. I insist that you stay here tonight. I will get the maids to make up a bed in one of the guest bed-chambers."

"That's very kind of you, Your Majesty," said the girl, who gave a little curtsy, and went off to have a steaming hot bath.

The Queen told her maids to collect as many mattresses and quilts as they could find and to stack them on the guest's bed. Then, she went to the castle kitchen where she picked out a single, dried pea from a jar. She gave the pea to one of the maids, and ordered that it be placed underneath the bottom mattress.

The girl's bed was now so tall she had to use a ladder to get into it!

In the morning, the Queen asked the girl if she'd had a good night's sleep. "Not really," replied the girl. "There was an annoying little lump in my bed that kept me awake all night."
This was just the reply that the Queen had been hoping for. Only a real Princess would have been able to feel a pea under all those mattresses and quilts.

When the Queen introduced her son to the Princess, they liked each other immediately.
"She's neither too short or too tall," the Prince told his parents. "Too fat or too thin. Too happy or too sad, or just plain old too nice! In fact, she's just perfect for me."

The Prince and the Princess got married, and the pea was put in a special case in the town's museum. For many years, the local people delighted in telling visitors the famous story of the Princess and the pea.

The Gingerbread Man

nce upon a time there was an old woman who decided to make some gingerbread. As she rolled out the dough, she noticed that she had a little bit left over.

"I'll make a gingerbread man out of this," she thought.

She cut the shape of a man out of the dough and used raisins for his eyes, nose and mouth.

"I'd better give him a jacket to wear," she thought. So she put raisins all down his front for buttons, too.

"There! That's not too bad," she said, looking at the little man proudly. Then she put him in the oven to bake, alongside the gingerbread.

A short time later, she heard a strange scratching sound coming from inside the oven and a little voice crying, "Help! Let me out of here!" She opened the oven door and, to her enormous surprise, out jumped the little gingerbread man.

"Thanks," he said. "It was getting very hot in there!"

Then he ran out of the kitchen door.

"Stop! Come back!" cried the old woman, chasing after him.

But the gingerbread man was far too quick for her. He looked back over his shoulder and said:

"Run, run, as fast as you can.
You can't catch me, I'm the gingerbread man!"

He ran into the garden where the old woman's husband was working. "Stop!" cried the old woman's husband and, with his arms outstretched, tried to grab the gingerbread man as he ran by. But the gingerbread man was far too quick for him, and said:

"Run, run, as fast as you can.
You can't catch me, I'm the gingerbread man!"

He ran further along the lane with the old woman and her husband chasing him.
Soon, he passed a cow who was eating some grass.
"Stop!' cried the cow. "Come back! You look good enough to eat!"
But the gingerbread man simply ran under the cow's legs and said:

"I've run from an old woman
and an old man.
Run, run, as fast as you can.
You can't catch me, I'm the gingerbread man!"

He ran further down the lane with the old woman, her husband and the cow chasing him.

A little later, he came across a horse in a field.

"Stop!' cried the horse. "Come back! You look good enough to eat!"

With one huge leap, the gingerbread man simply jumped right over the horse and laughed:

"I've run from an old woman
and an old man.
And a cow!
Run, run, as fast as you can.
You can't catch me, I'm the gingerbread man!"

He ran even further down the lane with the old woman,
her husband the cow and the horse chasing him.
When he passed some farmers making hay, they too cried,
"Stop! Come back! You look good enough to eat!"
But when they tried to grab him, the gingerbread man simply dived into
the pile of hay and came running out the other side.

"I've run from an old woman
and an old man.
And a cow and a horse!
Run, run, as fast as you can.
You can't catch me, I'm the gingerbread man!"

He ran much further down the lane, and then into a field, with the old
woman, her husband, the cow, the horse and the farmers all chasing him!
At the bottom of the field he met a fox and said to him:

"Run, run, as fast as you can.
You can't catch me, I'm the gingerbread man!"

But the fox was a sly, old thing who realized that he would have to be patient if he was going to catch the gingerbread man.

Soon after, the gingerbread man came to a river.

"Quick!" said the fox, who leapt out from behind a bush. "Jump on my back and I'll take you across, otherwise they'll catch you!"

The gingerbread man hopped onto the fox's back who then started to swim across the river. When they were halfway across, the water suddenly got deeper.

"You'd better sit on my head if you don't want to get wet!" the fox told the gingerbread man.

The gingerbread man did as he was told and hopped onto the fox's head.

A little further on, the water got deeper still.

"You'd better sit on my nose if you don't want to get wet!" said the fox to the gingerbread man.

The gingerbread man did as he was told and hopped onto the fox's nose. And that was the gingerbread man's big mistake. For as soon as he sat on the fox's nose, the fox opened his mouth, went snap and gobbled up the little gingerbread man straight away.

And, sadly, that was the end of the gingerbread man.

The Nightingale

ong ago, there lived in China an Emperor who liked to have only beautiful things around him. His palace was made of the most exquisite marble, his clothes were made of the finest silks and satins, his ornaments were made by the best craftsmen and his garden was the most glorious garden in his empire.

At the edge of the Emperor's garden flowed a river and on the bank grew a willow tree. Every evening at sunset, a nightingale would perch on one of its branches and sing its song to the sinking sun. Everyone who heard the nightingale's song thought it was the most beautiful sound in the world.

"If everyone thinks that this nightingale's song is the most beautiful sound in the world, why haven't I heard it sing?" asked the Emperor angrily. "Bring it to me, immediately!"

All the courtiers and palace guards ran around the garden in a panic trying to find the nightingale, but the garden was so big and the nightingale so small, it was impossible to find. After three days of looking, no one knew where to find the little bird.

"You're all fools!" yelled the Emperor at his soldiers. "You're supposed to be the finest soldiers in the world, and you can't even find a nightingale!"

"Excuse me, your Excellency, but I know where the nightingale lives," said a small voice behind him.

The Emperor turned around and saw that the small voice belonged to a little kitchen maid.

"He lives near me, close to the river," said the maid. "If you'd like me to, I could ask him to sing for you."

"I'd like that very much," said the Emperor, then collapsed in his chair, exhausted by all his shouting.

The little kitchen maid ran between the well-kept flower beds, over the small bridge on the lake and down through the soft, grassy meadows until she came to the river's edge.

"Are you there, nightingale?" she shouted up to the high branches of the trees.

"Yes, here I am," said the nightingale, sitting on a branch.

"His Excellency the Emperor would like you to sing to him tonight. What shall I tell him?"

"Tell the Emperor I'd be very pleased to sing for him," said the nightingale.

That evening, everyone in the palace waited silently with the Emperor to hear the bird sing. A window had been left open for the nightingale to fly into the room, and a special gold cushion for him to perch on had been placed next to the Emperor. With a flutter of tiny wings, the nightingale entered the grand hall through the window, perched on the gold cushion, opened its tiny mouth and began to sing. It was so beautiful that some people fainted and even the strongest of the guards had to wipe away their tears of joy.

The Emperor couldn't believe that this most precious bird had been
living in his garden, and he'd never known.

"From this day on, nightingale," the Emperor proclaimed. "You will be
a royal nightingale. You will have all the privileges a Prince would have.
You shall live in a golden cage, and have your own servants to care for
your every need. You will be able to take exercise but you will not be
able to leave the palace. All I ask is that you sing for me from time
to time."

The nightingale agreed to the Emperor's request and soon became the
most famous nightingale in China. He lived in great luxury, and many
people journeyed from far and wide to hear him sing.

One morning, a package arrived for the Emperor. It was a present from a friendly King. Inside was a beautiful toy nightingale that sang the sweetest song. It looked very pretty, as it was encrusted with diamonds, rubies and pearls. All the courtiers loved the toy bird. They thought it was even better than the real nightingale who would often tire after singing for a few hours. The toy bird could sing all night long. If it stopped, you just wound it up and it would start again.

The courtiers decided to hold a competition between the two nightingales to see which of the birds sang the best. The toy bird sang first. It sang for hours and, although it sang the same song over and over again, everybody agreed that the real nightingale would have to sing very well indeed if it was to beat the toy one. But the nightingale was nowhere to be found. Some of the soldiers in the courtyard below said they had seen it fly through an open window, away from the palace. The Emperor was very upset when he heard that the nightingale had escaped, but his courtiers told him that he was far better off with the toy one.

"It is far more suitable for your Excellency," they told him. "His song never tires and he is much prettier to look at."

The real nightingale was branded a traitor for leaving the Emperor's palace. In its place, the toy nightingale perched on the gold cushion each night and sang to the Emperor. And it sang for him for many years.

When the Emperor was old, he became ill and took to his bed. The only thing that gave him any comfort was the song of the toy nightingale. He had the bird placed next to him so he could listen to it whenever he wished.

One night, with a sudden, strange clanking sound the toy nightingale stopped singing. Something was very wrong. The finest toy engineers were brought to the palace to try to fix it, but they said that the poor bird's metal parts were completely worn out. It was impossible to repair. The toy nightingale had sung its last song.

Without its beautiful song to listen to, the Emperor's health became even worse, and it was feared that he would soon die. One night, as he lay in his bed thinking that this night might be his last, he heard the most beautiful music. He raised his head from the pillow and saw the real nightingale perched on his windowsill, singing its beautiful song.

"You've come back!" gasped the Emperor.
"I heard you were very ill," said the nightingale. "I thought if I sang for you, it might make you feel better."
"Your wonderful voice gives me hope and strength," said the Emperor, who was already starting to feel better. "You must come and live at the palace again," he continued excitedly. "There is nowhere in the world where you would be better cared for. Then I could listen to your lovely song every day."
"I'm sorry," said the nightingale. "I cannot live at the palace again. It is not the life for me. But I would be happy to come to your window and sing for you every night, if you so desire it."
"Oh, I do, I do!" cried the Emperor. "Thank you, nightingale. You have saved my life."

And from that night on, the nightingale perched on the Emperor's windowsill and sang for him, every night. The Emperor became strong again, and many people believed he became a kinder and wiser man.

Beauty and The Beast

Long ago, there lived a rich merchant who had three sons and three daughters. Unfortunately, his sons were only interested in hunting and fishing, while his two eldest daughters were greedy and selfish. Only his youngest daughter liked by everyone. Everyone called her "Beauty". Not only was she very beautiful to look at, she but was the kindest person that anyone had ever met.

One day, the merchant heard some terrible news. All the ships carrying his goods had sunk at sea in a storm, which left him with hardly any money. The whole family had to move from their grand house to a little cottage. While the merchant and his sons worked hard all day in the fields, his daughters stayed at home doing the housework. The two eldest daughters were very lazy and sat around doing nothing. Beauty, however, enjoyed her work around the cottage, happy to be helping her father in these difficult times.

One morning, a letter arrived for the merchant. It said that one of his ships had not sunk and it was going to arrive at the port the following morning.
"Maybe we're not so poor, after all!" said the merchant, happily. With great excitement, he set off to meet his ship. Before he left, he asked his daughters what they would like as gifts. The eldest daughters asked for jewels and beautiful clothes but Beauty, who didn't have a greedy bone in her body, simply asked for a single red rose.

When the merchant got to the port he found out that there had been a terrible mistake. There was no ship coming into port, which meant that he was just as poor as before. The unhappy man turned his horse around and set off for home again.

Later that night, there was a huge storm. Thunder and lightening filled the sky, and the poor merchant lost his way in the darkness. He was soon soaked to the skin and his horse was getting very tired.
At last, he saw lights in the distance. Getting closer, he realized that the lights shone from a castle. He rode up to the castle, and knocked on the door. It creaked open.

Inside, he found a roaring fire and food on the table, but only one plate. There was no one else around, so he sat down and ate. After he'd eaten, he went outside and discovered a stable in the courtyard. It was bright and warm with lots of hay for his horse to eat and clean straw for it to sleep on. Back in the castle, he ventured upstairs. One of the bedrooms was warm, with freshly ironed sheets laid out on the bed.

"It's almost as if I was expected," thought the merchant, before climbing into bed and falling fast asleep.

When he awoke the next morning, he got dressed and went downstairs.
Again, breakfast was neatly laid out on the table. Again, nobody else
was around. After he'd eaten, he saddled his horse. Riding out of the
long drive, he noticed a rosebush with beautiful, red flowers.
"At least I can give Beauty the present she asked for," he thought, and
plucked a single red rose from the bush.

From out of the bushes, an ugly looking Beast appeared in front of him.
"You eat my food, sleep in my guest room and now you want to steal
one of my roses. You shall die for this!"
The terrified merchant stuttered back, "But I didn't see anyone to
thank. And I was only taking this one rose for Beauty."
"Who is this Beauty?" demanded the Beast.
"She is my daughter," replied the merchant.
The Beast thought for a moment.
"Very well, then," he said. "You may leave here on the condition that
your daughter, Beauty, takes your place and comes to me here."
The merchant was so scared, he hastily agreed and rode out of the
castle grounds as quickly as possible.

When he arrived home, he told his family what had happened.
"I can't possibly let you go," he told Beauty through his tears. "The
Beast might kill you!"
"You have to, father," said Beauty calmly. "If I don't go, he might take
revenge on our family."
Sadly, the merchant agreed that he had to let Beauty go. With a heavy
heart, he waved her farewell as she set out for the Beast's castle.

When she got there, she found to her great surprise that the Beast was very kind to her. He showed her around the castle and its beautiful grounds and then took her to her room. The Beast had made sure that all the books she'd like to read and all the little ornaments she'd like to look at were there. There was even a magic mirror in which she could see her family back at home. The scene lasted a few seconds before it faded away.

"This Beast may be ugly, but he is very considerate," thought Beauty.

On that first evening, the Beast came to eat supper with her. After the meal, he asked her to marry him.

"I'm sorry, but I cannot marry you," she replied.

The Beast sighed, and then slowly walked out of the room.

From then on, it was the same every evening. Beauty and the Beast would have supper together and then he'd ask her to marry him. Beauty always gave the same reply: "I'm sorry, but I cannot marry you."

Time passed. Then, one evening, Beauty looked into the mirror and saw that her father was very ill. She begged the Beast to allow her to go home and care for him.

"Very well," said the Beast. "But you must return here within a week. When you are ready to come back, put this ring on your dressing table at home and I shall know you want to return here. If you don't do this within one week, I shall die."

Beauty agreed, and when she woke up the next morning, she found herself in her own bed at home.

She cared for her father day and night over the next few days, and soon one week had passed. Although her father was getting better, Beauty had been so busy, she hadn't noticed how quickly the days had passed. To make matters worse, her older sisters who had always been jealous of her, didn't tell her. They were secretly hoping that the longer she stayed at home, the angrier the Beast would become.

"He might even kill her!" they chuckled to themselves.

One night, Beauty had a dream that the Beast was lying dead by the side of the lake in his castle grounds.

"I must go back to him," she thought. She put the ring he gave her on her dressing table, and the next morning found herself back in his castle. She ran down to the lake and was horrified to see that the Beast was lying on the ground, barely alive.

"Oh, Beast," she cried, "I did not mean to stay away so long. Please come back to me. You are so good and kind."

Then, she kissed him.

Suddenly, the Beast changed right in front of her eyes. All signs of his ugliness had disappeared and there was a handsome prince in his place. "Beauty, my love," explained the Prince. "I had a spell cast on me many years ago that turned me into an ugly beast. The only way it could be broken was if a girl who loved me, kissed me in spite of my ugliness." Beauty kissed him again and vowed that she would stay by his side forever.

The happy couple rode to her father's house where they were married. Then they journeyed back to the castle where they lived in complete happiness for many years to come.

Aladdin's Lamp

A long time ago in faraway China, there lived a poor tailor, his wife and their son, Aladdin. The tailor worked hard and hoped that his son would one day enter the family business. But all Aladdin liked to do was spend time with his friends. Even when his father died, Aladdin didn't stop being lazy. It was left to his poor old mother to bring a little money into the house by spinning cotton.

One day, while he was lazing around as usual, a stranger approached Aladdin and said, "My goodness, but you must be Aladdin. You look just like your father! I am your father's brother who has been away for many years. Please take me to your mother at once."
Aladdin was surprised. He didn't think he had an uncle but did as he was told, anyway. When his mother saw the stranger she was also confused and said, "Yes, my husband did have a brother. I never met him. I thought he died many years ago."
But it was such a happy meeting and the stranger seemed such a nice man, she found it easy to believe that it was her dead husband's brother.

What Aladdin and his mother didn't know was that the stranger was an evil magician who had picked Aladdin because he looked like a wastrel. He wanted to use Aladdin for his own ends and then get rid of him. However, for the time being, he was very charming to the boy and his mother.

After treating them to a good meal, the magician told the boy he'd like to show him around the richer parts of the city. They walked through beautiful gardens and wide streets with magnificent houses. After a while, Aladdin and the magician found themselves in a small, dark alley. Without warning, the magician stopped and pulled on a big metal ring attached to a flat stone in the middle of the street. Underneath the stone were stairs, leading down into darkness.

"Nephew," began the magician. "You must go down these stairs for me. At the bottom you will find three caves full of gold and silver. You must pass through all of the caves and promise not to touch anything! Then you will enter a garden full of strange stone-fruit hanging from the trees. You may pick some of it if you wish. At the end of the garden you will find a dirty old lamp. Empty the oil from it and bring it to me. The lamp is the only thing I wish for."

Aladdin was a little nervous, but the magician had given him a beautiful emerald ring to keep if he promised to bring the lamp back. Aladdin went slowly down the stairs. At the bottom, he found the three caves that were full of gold and silver, just as his uncle had said. But he kept his promise and didn't touch any of it.

Then he entered the garden with the strange stone-fruit hanging from the trees. He stuffed as many as he could into his pockets, then carried on until he reached the end of the garden. There, he saw the old oil lamp. He picked it up, poured out the old, dirty oil and walked back through the garden and the three caves until he reached the stairs again.

The magician was waiting for him at the top of the stairs.

"Give me the lamp!" he said eagerly.

"Help me out of here first, and then I'll give you the lamp," said Aladdin.

"I want it now!" cried the magician, and tried to grab the lamp out of Aladdin's hand. This had been his plan all along. He was going to take the lamp, then shut Aladdin beneath the ground forever. But as the two of them struggled, the stone suddenly fell back over the hole, shutting Aladdin, with the lamp, firmly inside.

The magician quickly realized that his plan had failed, and left China, never to be seen again.

For two days Aladdin stayed in the cave without any food and water. He was getting very weak. Then, by chance, he rubbed the ring the magician had given him. All of a sudden, there was a blinding flash and a very large man appeared in front of him.

"Who are you?" asked Aladdin in astonishment.

"I am the Genie of the Ring, master. Your wish is my command. What can I do for you?"

"Get me out of here!" cried Aladdin.

There was another blinding flash and Aladdin found himself standing in the alley above. Looking down, he saw that the big metal ring and the flat stone had completely disappeared. He rushed home to his mother, who was overjoyed to see him.

"Where have you been, my boy?" she asked, hugging him.

"I'll tell you later," said Aladdin. "I'm so hungry. I haven't eaten for two days. Please feed me, mother."

His mother cooked up whatever bits she had in the house, but it wasn't very much and, after he'd finished eating, Aladdin was still hungry.

"Maybe I can sell the lamp for food," he said. "I'd better give it a polish."
As soon as he started to rub the lamp, there was another blinding flash
and another large man appeared!

Both Aladdin and his mother cried out in amazement.

"Who are you?" asked Aladdin in a trembling voice.

"I am the Genie of the Lamp, master," said the large man. "Your wish is
my command. What can I do for you?"

"Bring me a table full of food," commanded Aladdin.

In the blink of an eye, a table appeared crammed full of the most
delicious food, all served up on silver plates. When Aladdin and his
mother had eaten everything, they sold the silver plates for a lot of
money, which bought them enough food not to go hungry again for a
very long time.

One day, while strolling in the market, Aladdin saw the Sultan's
daughter, Princess Badroulboudoir, and fell in love with her instantly.
He went to see the Sultan and asked for his daughter's hand in
marriage. As a gift, Aladdin gave the Sultan all of the stone-fruit he'd
found hanging from the trees in the cave.

"You must be very rich to give me such a present," smiled the Sultan.
"You're exactly the sort of man I wish my daughter to marry."

But the Sultan's chief courtier wanted his son to marry the Princess, so
he urged the Sultan to give Aladdin a test to prove himself. So the Sultan
asked Aladdin for even more of the stone-fruit. But this time the Sultan
wanted forty servants to carry the fruit to his palace on forty
silver platters.

When he was alone, Aladdin once again rubbed the lamp, and again the
Genie appeared.

"What can I do for you, master?" he asked Aladdin.
"Send forty servants, bearing forty platters of stone-fruit, to the Sultan's palace," ordered Aladdin.

The Sultan was astonished when, the very next day, forty servants bearing forty platters of fruit arrived at his palace.
"Look at this!" exclaimed the Sultan. "I am now certain that Aladdin will make a fine husband for my daughter."
But the chief courtier, who still had hopes that his son might marry the Sultan's daughter, suggested one final test for Aladdin.
"This is all well and good," he said. "But where would they live if they were married? If Aladdin is as wealthy as he says he is, he should be able to build a wonderful new palace for your daughter."

"You're right," said the Sultan, who was a simple man at heart and always thought that his chief courtier knew best. He told Aladdin that he could definitely marry his daughter if he built her a marvellous palace to live in. Aladdin summoned the Genie once again, and once again the Genie did his magic.

Shortly after, a brand new palace appeared right next door to where the Sultan lived. It was the finest palace anybody had ever seen. The walls were covered with gold and silver and every room was filled with fabulous treasures. Aladdin and the Princess had a huge wedding and lived a long and happy life. Aladdin never forgot the secret of his happiness and made sure to keep his lamp safe for the rest of his days.

Rapunzel

There was once a man and his wife who lived in a small house at the edge of a forest that overlooked a beautiful garden. There were all sorts of unusual plants and pretty flowers growing in the garden, and the man and his wife liked nothing better than to sit out on a summer's afternoon enjoying the magnificent view.

As much as they liked looking at the garden, they were not allowed to go in it. The garden belonged to a witch who forbade anyone but her to enter it. One day, the man's wife announced to her husband that she was going to have a baby. Not long after, she became very ill. She lay in bed, refused to eat and got thinner and thinner. Her husband was beside himself with worry.

"There's only one thing that can help me," she told her husband in a tired voice.

"And what is that, my dear?" her husband asked, eager to help in any way he could.

"There is a strange herb growing in the witch's garden, called rapunzel. If you can get some for me, it will make me well again."

That night, the man quietly tiptoed into the garden and made his way to where the rapunzel herb grew. He bent down and started to pick the ripe, green leaves.

"How dare you steal my herbs!" a voice suddenly rang out in the darkness. "You shall suffer for this!" It was the witch, who stood towering over the poor man with an evil look on her face.

"Oh, please," he stammered. "I didn't mean any harm. But my wife is very ill and the only thing that will make her better are the leaves of the rapunzel herb."

"I see," said the witch, thinking for a moment. "All right," she finally said. "You may take as much rapunzel as you wish, but only on the condition that when your child is born, you must hand the infant over to me."

It was a difficult choice to make but, fearing that his wife might die, the poor man agreed to the witch's demand.

After eating the rapunzel leaves, the man's wife did get well again and a few months later, she gave birth to a beautiful baby girl. No sooner had the couple wrapped their child in a blanket than the witch appeared to claim her prize.

"I believe this child is mine. I think I'll call her Rapunzel, after the herb that you stole from my garden," she cackled loudly.

She grabbed the baby from her mother's arms and whisked her away into the forest.

As Rapunzel grew up, the witch made sure she neither saw nor spoke to any other living person. Fearing that she might try to escape, the witch put Rapunzel at the top of a tall tower that lay deep in the forest. There were no stairs, only one small window and no door. Despite these harsh conditions, Rapunzel seemed happy enough, singing to herself all day long, and feeding the little birds that came to sit on her windowsill with small crumbs of bread.

Rapunzel had never had her beautiful hair cut, so by the time she was put in the tower, her hair was thick, golden and very, very long. Once a day, the witch delivered Rapunzel's food. She'd stand at the bottom of the tower and call up.
"Rapunzel, Rapunzel! Let down your golden hair."
Rapunzel would throw down her plaited hair that reached right to the bottom of the tower. Then the witch would climb steadily up. After the witch had delivered her food, she climbed down the same golden rope.

One day, a young Prince was riding through the forest. As he rode, he heard someone singing nearby. The voice was so lovely, and the song was so beautiful, he decided to find out where it came from. It seemed to be coming from a tall tower that stood nearby. The Prince got off his horse and looked for a door. But, after searching thoroughly, he could find no entrance to the tower.

Just then he heard footsteps behind him. He hid behind a bush and saw a witch walking towards the tower with a tray of food. When she got there, she called up.
"Rapunzel, Rapunzel! Let down your golden hair."
A long plait of golden hair fell from the small window at the top of the tower. The witch began to climb up slowly.

A short while later, the witch climbed down the hair-rope and disappeared into the forest.

"So, that's the way in," thought the Prince. He went to the foot of the tower and called up.

"Rapunzel, Rapunzel! Let down your golden hair." The hair came cascading down and the Prince began to climb up. When he reached the top, he found that the hair belonged to a beautiful girl. She told him that her name was Rapunzel. They liked each other very much and talked for hours. When it was time for him to leave, he said to her, "I wish I could take you with me."

"I wish so, too," said Rapunzel. "But that can never be. Please leave now. I don't know what the witch would do to us if she were to find you here."

The Prince climbed back down Rapunzel's hair, vowing that he would see her again.

The next time that the witch climbed up the hair, Rapunzel winced. "Ouch," she cried. And before she could stop herself she said, "Why can't you be more gentle, like the Prince who came to see me?"

When the witch realized that someone else had been to see Rapunzel, she went blue in the face with anger.

"How dare you talk to somebody else," she screamed. She grabbed Rapunzel by her hair and dragged her out of the tower and into the deepest, darkest part of the forest. Then she cut off her hair and left the poor girl sobbing on the forest floor.

The next day, the Prince returned to the tower.

"Rapunzel, Rapunzel! Let down your golden hair," he called up. The hair dropped down and the Prince climbed up. Once at the top, he didn't find Rapunzel but the witch who had tied Rapunzel's hair around the windowsill.

"So," she cackled softly. "You're the young man who has been tempting Rapunzel away."

Before he could answer, the witch leaped on him with a great scream and pushed him out of the window. Luckily, he landed softly in a thorn bush. But the thorns had scratched his eyes so much that he could hardly see. He stumbled deeper into the forest, not knowing where he was going.

After wandering around for hours, the Prince heard the faint sound of singing. He let himself be guided by the voice which led him straight to Rapunzel.

"Oh, my poor Prince," she said. "How happy I am to see you. But what has happened to your eyes?"
After he'd told her how the witch had thrown him out of the tower, Rapunzel gently bathed his eyes in the waters of a nearby stream. She then squeezed the juice of a special berry into them that would help make them better.

When the Prince was well enough, he and Rapunzel found their way out of the forest and back to his castle. They were married at once and lived happily ever after. The Prince's father, the King, banished the wicked witch from his land forever and she was never seen or heard of again.

The Tortoise and The Hare

On summer evenings, all the woodland animals used to meet in a beautiful, shaded clearing. They talked to each other about the day's events, played games among the trees or just lazed about, enjoying the last rays of the sun.

The fastest animal in the wood was Hare. He loved running and always won when the animals decided to have a game of tag. No one ever caught him! The slowest animal in the wood was Tortoise. He plodded along very slowly on his four little feet, often arriving at the clearing at sunset, as the other animals were ready to leave.

"Here he comes," the other animals would say. "Perhaps, if he took his shell off his back, he might move a bit faster!"
Tortoise didn't really mind their teasing. He was a cheerful soul who wasn't at all bothered that he was the slowest animal in the wood. He was happiest of all when chewing on a tasty, fresh leaf.

One warm summer's evening, the animals were gathered in the clearing, chatting and lying around. As usual, Tortoise was the last to arrive.
"Watch out! Here he comes!" said Fox. "Get out of the way everyone, or you might be run down!"
Everybody laughed at Fox's joke and went back to what they were doing.

But this evening was a little different than usual. Tortoise slowly made his way to Hare, who was chatting to a group of friends.

When Tortoise got there, he said, "Excuse me Hare, but do you think you are the fastest animal in the wood?"

"I don't think that I'm the fastest animal in the wood . . . I know I am," said Hare, smugly.

"That's very interesting," said Tortoise. "Because I'm certain that I could beat you if we were to have a race."

"You . . . beat me?" replied an astonished Hare, and fell to the ground in an uncontrollable fit of laughter. "But you're the slowest animal in the world. You can't possibly beat me!"

"Well, if you're frightened of running against me, I perfectly understand," said Tortoise, and slowly began to walk away.

"Wait a minute," said Hare, a little irritated. "I'm not frightened of running against you. I'm just telling you that you don't stand a chance. But, if you insist on looking like a fool . . . when would you like to race?"

"Let's meet here in the morning," said Tortoise.

The next morning, all the animals gathered in the clearing to watch the start of this most peculiar race. Tortoise and Hare lined up behind the start line.

"Right," said Fox. "You will race around the woodland path and back to the clearing where the finish line will be. Whoever crosses it first will be the winner. Do you understand?"

Hare and Tortoise nodded.

"On your marks, get set, go!" cried Fox.

Hare set off as fast as he could. He ran so quickly that, after a few seconds, he'd completely disappeared from view. Tortoise plodded along at a snail's pace, putting one foot slowly in front of the other.

Tortoise's friends groaned. "This contest is over almost before it has begun," they thought.

"Move a little bit faster," they urged.

"Don't worry," replied Tortoise. "I may be very slow, but I'll still win this race."

THE TORTOISE AND THE HARE

Far ahead, Hare was still tearing along at top speed. Looking back over his shoulder, he saw that there was no sign of Tortoise.

"What an idiot I am," he thought. "Why am I running so fast? I'm a long way in front of Tortoise. I could walk all the way and I'd still beat him."

Just then he heard a voice. It was his friend, Badger.

"Hi, Hare. What's going on?" asked Badger.

"I'm in a race with Tortoise," replied Hare.

"With tortoise?" exclaimed Badger with a surprised look on his face. Then he exploded into laughter.

"Well, you've got plenty of time. It'll take him hours to get to the finish line. I've found some beautiful fresh berries," he continued. "Come share them with me."

Hare was feeling a bit hungry so, after looking down the track to make sure Tortoise was still nowhere in sight, he sat down with Badger to enjoy the delicious berries.

When they had finished eating, Hare stood up and stretched.

"Thanks, Badger," he said. "Those berries were lovely, but I'd better get on my way."

"Don't worry," laughed Badger. "Tortoise is a long way behind. I'd take it easy if I were you."

"You're right," grinned Hare. "He'll be hours, yet. There's no point in wearing myself out."

Hare waved goodbye to Badger and walked leisurely along the path. It was a beautiful day and he could feel the warm sun on his back. After a while, he began to feel a little sleepy.

"I think I might just lie down and shut my eyes for a few minutes," Hare thought. He found a lovely, mossy bank to lie on by the river, gave a big contented yawn and, a few moments later, was fast asleep.

But Tortoise hadn't stopped to eat with anybody, and he hadn't decided to have a sleep, either. After some time, Tortoise passed the sleeping Hare and plodded slowly on towards the clearing. The other animals couldn't believe their eyes when they saw Tortoise making his way slowly towards the finish line.

"But what has happened to Hare?" they wondered. He was nowhere in sight!

At that very moment, Hare woke up with a sudden start.

"Oh, no!" he thought. " I must have been sleeping for hours. I'd better hurry!"

He ran along the path as fast as he could, but it was too late. Tortoise was just crossing the finish line as Hare ran into the clearing.

All the animals gathered around Tortoise, patting him on his shell and congratulating him.

"Congratulations, Tortoise!" said Fox. "Nobody really thought that you could race Hare and actually win. But you did just that!"

"You've beaten me," said Hare, breathlessly. "I don't believe it."

"I told you I would, didn't I?" grinned Tortoise. "Remember, slow and steady will always win the day."

Then he plodded slowly off to enjoy a well-deserved meal of fresh, green leaves.

Sleeping Beauty

There once were a King and Queen who seemed to have everything anyone could wish for. They lived in a beautiful palace and ruled over a happy country where all their subjects loved them dearly. But there was one thing that made the King and Queen very sad indeed: they had no children.

One morning, as the King was looking over some documents with his courtiers, the Queen suddenly burst in.

"My dear," she said breathlessly, "I have great news!"

"And what might that be, my love?" asked the King.

"I'm going to have a baby!" exclaimed the Queen, excitedly.

The King was so delighted he dropped his map, burst into tears and gave his wife a great big hug.

A few months later, the Queen gave birth to a little girl. And she was the prettiest baby anyone had ever seen. She had big blue eyes, lovely blonde hair and a perfect smile. The King was so taken with his child, he ordered a national holiday on the day she was born. He and the Queen adored their new daughter and spent many hours gazing lovingly at her.

"She's as beautiful as you, my dear," said the King fondly to the Queen.

"I'm sure she'll grow up to be as wise as you," the Queen replied.

"Thank you, my love. How blessed we are," said the King.

The King decided to hold a huge christening party for the new Princess, and invited people from far and wide. When the great day came, everyone in the palace was very excited. The cooks had been up all night preparing delicious food, the royal gardeners had been working for weeks to make the palace grounds look perfect and the sentries had polished their buttons so hard, they gleamed like gold.

Everybody had a wonderful time! After the great feast, the King clapped his hands and the music and dancing began.

The King and Queen also invited six fairies to the christening party, whom they hoped would bestow special gifts on the new Princess.

When all the guests had exhausted themselves on the dance floor, it was time for the fairies to bestow their gifts on the newborn Princess. One by one, they approached her crib.

"I bestow beauty on you," said the first fairy, gazing fondly down at the gurgling Princess.

"Joy," said the second.

"Wisdom," said the third.

"To be generous," said the fourth.

"Health," said the fifth.

But before the sixth fairy could bestow her gifts, the doors of the great chamber were suddenly flung open. There stood an old, ugly fairy that no one really liked, and were secretly a little afraid of.

"Why wasn't I invited to your party?" the old fairy asked, glaring at the King.

"Well … I … umm, I'm not quite sure," stuttered the King, looking down at his shoes, feeling embarrassed.

Everyone fell silent.

"I have a gift I'd like to bestow on the dear child." said the old fairy, walking up to the crib and looking down at the Princess.

"My gift to you," she began, "is that when you reach the age of sixteen, you will prick yourself on the spindle of spinning wheel and you will die!"

And with that, she turned around and walked angrily out of the palace.

The poor Queen burst into tears. Then a lovely, clear voice rang out. It was the sixth fairy.

"I haven't bestowed my gift yet," she said. "I cannot undo the terrible curse of the old fairy but I can change it a little. My gift to you, little one, is that you won't die if you prick your finger on a spindle but, instead, you will sleep for one hundred years."

From that day on, the King banned all use of spinning wheels. If people wanted any wool to be spun, they had to send it to another land.

Time passed, and everyone started to forget the old fairy and her curse. The Princess grew up to be beautiful, healthy, wise and generous. Everyone in the country loved her.

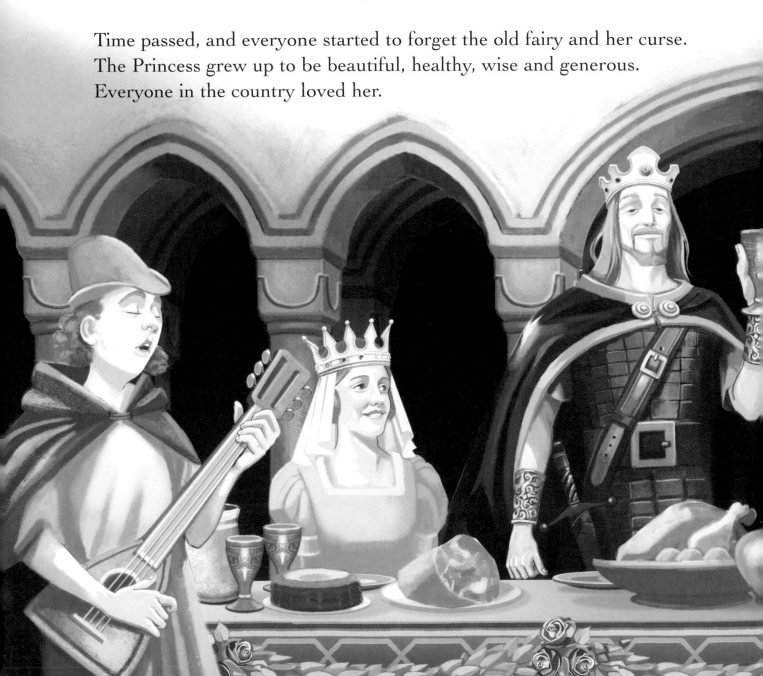

On her sixteenth birthday, the King gave a grand party. For a present, he had a beautiful dress made for her. It was the first proper grown up dress the Princess had ever worn. It was a lovely, green silk dress, with an elegant, high collar, and it was so long it reached the floor.

The Princess invited all her friends to the party. After eating a huge birthday lunch, they decided to play hide-and-seek.
"You won't catch me," said the Princess, running quickly away.
Trying to find a place where nobody would find her, she climbed a stone staircase to the very top of one of the palace's towers.

At the top was a small room. Inside the room, an old lady sat at her spinning wheel. She had been there for years, and hadn't heard that spinning wheels had been banned long ago.

"How nice to see you, my dear," said the old lady with a warm smile.

"What beautiful thread you're making!" exclaimed the Princess. "May I try the spinning wheel?"

She sat down at the wheel and began to spin but, as soon as she did so, the spindle pricked her finger.

With a small cry, she fell to the ground and fell fast asleep.

At that very moment, everybody else in the palace, and in the palace grounds, fell asleep too.

Many years went by and, little by little, a huge thorn hedge grew around the palace. It was so thick that the few people who tried to fight their way through gave up. In time, the palace, and the people sleeping in it, were completely forgotten.

Then, one day, a Prince from a far off land rode by and saw one of the palace's gleaming towers in the distance. In a nearby village, he asked if anybody knew to whom it belonged. But nobody did. It was too long ago. Then, a very old man said his grandfather had told him that, many years ago, a palace had stood there, but no one had been able to cut through the thorn hedge to get to it.

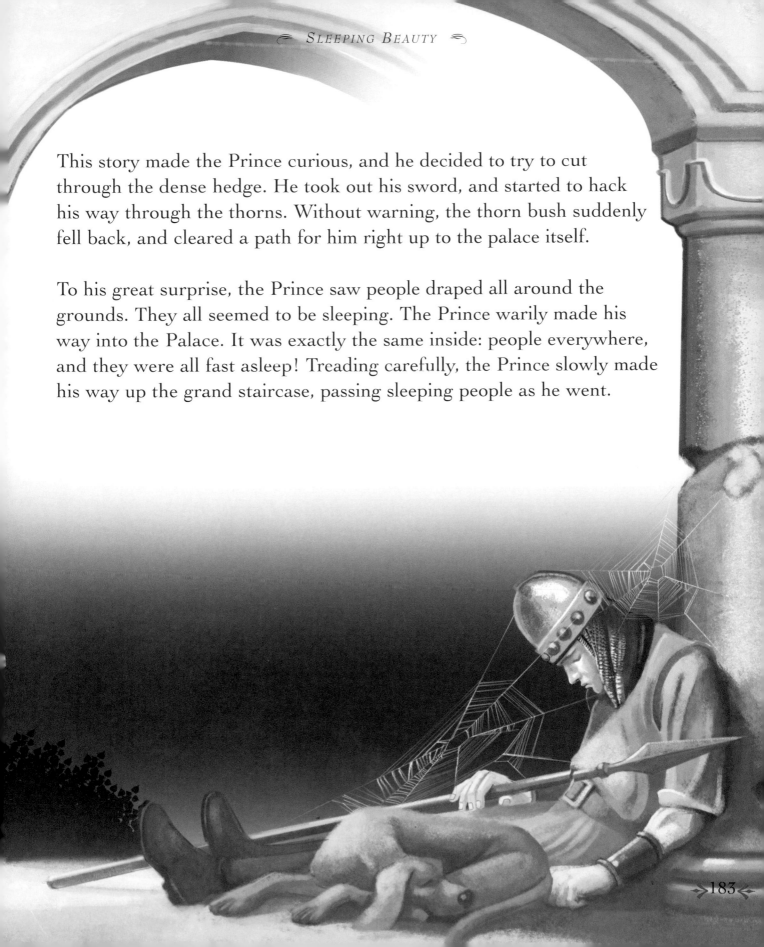

This story made the Prince curious, and he decided to try to cut through the dense hedge. He took out his sword, and started to hack his way through the thorns. Without warning, the thorn bush suddenly fell back, and cleared a path for him right up to the palace itself.

To his great surprise, the Prince saw people draped all around the grounds. They all seemed to be sleeping. The Prince warily made his way into the Palace. It was exactly the same inside: people everywhere, and they were all fast asleep! Treading carefully, the Prince slowly made his way up the grand staircase, passing sleeping people as he went.

At the top of the stairs was a large oak door. He pushed it open and couldn't believe his eyes. In front of him lay a lovely Princess who was also sound asleep. She was so beautiful, he gasped out loud. In one swift movement, the Prince knelt by her side and kissed her gently on the lips. To his utter astonishment, her eyes slowly opened, and she began to wake. The Prince looked into her deep blue eyes and realized she was the girl he had been waiting for all his life.

At that moment, everyone else in the palace woke up, too. It was exactly one hundred years since the old fairy had cast her evil curse. When they realized what had happened all those years before, everyone was so happy to be alive.

The Prince and Princess decided to marry. The palace was cleaned of its cobwebs and their wedding took place soon after. It was a joyous day for everyone and the Prince and Princess lived happily ever after.

Rumpelstiltskin

Once upon a time there was on old woman who lived with her beautiful daughter in a run-down old cottage. The woman and the girl were very poor and it was always hard to find enough to eat. One day, the old woman happened to see the King riding along the road by her cottage.

"If only I could arrange for the King to meet my daughter," she thought. "She's so beautiful, he might even marry her."

She grabbed hold of the King's horse and pulled it to a stop.

"Please, sire, you must meet my daughter. She is very beautiful."

"You stupid woman. Get out of my way before I whip you!" cried the King, nearly falling off his horse.

"But she can do something that would make you very rich," the woman said, desperately trying to hold his attention.

"Oh, and what is that?" asked the King, with curiosity.

The old woman said the first thing that came into her head.

"She can spin straw into gold," she lied.

The King took the old woman's daughter, whose name was Rose, to his castle. He locked her up in a small room that was full of straw. The only other things in the room were a spinning wheel and a small stool.

"Listen to me, Rose," the King began. "I will return in the morning. If all this straw has not been turned into gold, I will chop your pretty little head off. Good night!" Then he walked out of the room, locking the door behind him.

Poor Rose was so afraid she started to cry. Just then, she noticed a funny little man with a long, grey beard standing at her elbow.

"What's the matter, my dear?" asked the funny little man.

"My stupid mother told the King that I can spin straw into gold," cried Rose. If I can't do it, the King will have my head chopped off . . . and I can't do it!"

"I can," said the funny little man. "What would you give me if I did it for you?"

"My necklace," replied Rose, taking it from her neck.

"That will do fine," said the little man, putting it in his pocket. "You have a rest and I'll get on with my work."

The little man sat down and started to spin. The last thing Rose heard before she fell asleep was the whirr of the spinning wheel as it went round and round and round.

The next morning, with the sun streaming in through the window, Rose awoke. She rubbed her eyes and couldn't believe what she saw. There was no sign of the funny little man but all the straw in the room had been turned into the finest gold. The King was very pleased when he saw it all.

"You've done very well, Rose," he said. "Now, come with me."

This time he took her to an even bigger room which, again, was full of straw.

"I want all of this spun into gold by the morning or I'll chop your head off!" threatened the King.

Once again, he left Rose alone in the room and locked the door behind him.

"What am I going to do?" thought Rose, and she began to cry again.

"Don't cry," said a voice at her elbow. "I'll turn it all into gold for you. But what will you give me in return?"

It was the funny little man again, who had just appeared from nowhere!

"Here, take my ring. It was my grandmother's," said Rose, pulling it off her finger.

The little man put the ring in his pocket, sat at the wheel and began to spin.

The next morning, it was the same as before. The little man had gone and all of the straw had been turned into gold. When the King saw this, he took Rose to a very large room that had straw piled up to the ceiling. "If you manage to turn all of this into gold, I'll make you my Queen," he said. "If you don't, it's off with your head!"

After the King had left, the funny little man appeared once more, and once more offered to turn all the straw into gold.

"But I have nothing left to give you," said poor Rose.

"There is one thing you can give me. You can give me your first born baby," said the little man, slyly. "If you make me this promise, I will turn all of this straw into gold."

Rose was so desperate, she agreed to his demand at once.

When the King saw the huge amount of gold in the room the next
morning, he was so pleased that he married Rose immediately. A year
later, she gave birth to a lovely, little baby boy.

In time, Rose forgot about her promise to the little man but, one
evening, when she was all alone nursing her baby, he suddenly appeared
at her elbow.

"I have come to claim the baby you promised me," he said, with a cold
look in his eye.

Rose was horrified and promised the little man anything he wanted:
jewels, gold, anything. As long as he didn't take her child away.

The little man thought for a moment and then said, "I will give you a
chance to keep your child. I will come here for the next three nights and
each night I will give you three chances to guess my name. If you don't
guess correctly by the third night, you will never see your baby again."

When the little man appeared on the first night, Rose tried to think of
three of the most unusual names.

"Is it Caspar?" she asked.

"No," replied the little man.

"Is it Balthasar?" she asked, anxiously.

"I'm afraid not," he replied with an evil grin.

"What about Melchior?" she asked, even more anxiously.

"Wrong, wrong, wrong!" he cried, gleefully. Then he stamped his foot
and disappeared.

The next evening, Rose thought that she'd try more ordinary names.

"Is it John?"

"No," replied the little man.

"Arthur?" she asked again.

"Not even close," he replied.

"How about George?" asked Rose.

"Wrong, wrong, wrong again!" he shouted, happily.

Once again, Rose had failed.

The little man was so pleased that Rose couldn't guess his name, he started to dance around the room with joy.

"If you don't guess my name tomorrow night," he cried, "the child is mine!" Then he stamped his foot and disappeared.

Early the next morning, Rose sent all her servants out to see if they could find anyone who had heard of the little man and knew his name. One by one the servants came back. They could find no one who had heard of him. Finally, the last servant arrived back and had a strange tale to tell Rose.

"I was riding through the forest," he said, "and I saw a strange little man with a long, grey beard dancing around his fire. He sang a strange song, too."

"Today I brew, tomorrow I bake.
Next day, Queen Rose's baby I'll take.
So I solemnly swear by the hair on my chin,
That the name I was given is Rumpelstiltskin."

Rose was so delighted with this news, she gave the servant a large bag of gold coins as a reward. Later that evening, the little man once again appeared in front of her.

"What are your last three guesses?" he asked Rose, smugly.

"Is it Karl?" she asked.

"No," he replied, happily.

"Umm . . . Richard?" she asked again.

"Nowhere near, I'm afraid. It's your last guess, Your Majesty, and then the child is mine," the little man said, menacingly.

"Is it . . . Rumpelstiltskin?" asked Rose, innocently.

The little man was so angry that Rose had guessed his name, he turned bright blue. He stamped his foot down so hard that he went right through the floor, and that was the end of Rumpelstiltskin.

Hansel and Gretel

here was once a woodcutter and his wife who lived in a tiny cottage, on the edge of a magnificent forest, with their two children. They had a boy called Hansel and a girl called Gretel. It was a hard life and there never seemed to be enough food.

In one particularly lean year, the woodcutter's wife turned to her husband one night. "There's not enough bread for us all tomorrow," she said. "It would be best for everyone if you took the children into the forest and left them there."
"But they'll starve to death!" exclaimed the woodcutter.
"It's either them or us," replied his heartless wife.
The woodcutter tried to make his wife change her mind, but after much argument, he reluctantly agreed to leave his children in the forest the following day.

Meanwhile, Hansel had overheard his mother and father arguing. When he heard of their terrible plan, he crept outside, picked up some white pebbles and put them in his pocket. Early the next morning, the woodcutter told his children that they must help carry the wood that he was going to chop down that day. As they walked deeper into the forest, Hansel began to drop behind him the pebbles he had collected.
"What are you doing?" Gretel asked him.
"Sshh! You'll find out," replied her brother.

After walking for many hours, the woodcutter told his children to rest while he started to cut down the trees. The children were tired after walking so far and slowly drifted off to sleep on the forest floor. When they awoke, it was night, and very dark. They realized that their father had left them in the forest, completely alone.

"I'm frightened," said Gretel, clutching her brother's arm.
"Don't worry," said Hansel. "Do you remember those white pebbles I dropped on the way here? If we follow them, they'll lead us home."
Sure enough, the children followed the trail of white pebbles that gleamed in the dark, and they arrived home just as the sun had started to lighten the sky.

Their father was overjoyed to see them and hugged them tightly. He hadn't wanted to leave them in the forest in the first place. But their mother was not at all pleased to see them, and packed them off to bed as quickly as possible. That night, she told her husband that the next day he was to take the children even further into the forest and leave them there again. The poor woodcutter tried to argue with her but she refused to change her mind.

Early the next morning, Hansel and Gretel's mother gave them each a chunk of bread and told them that they must help their father in the forest again. This time, clever Hansel tore off little bits of the bread and dropped them behind him as they walked along the path.

"See," he whispered to his sister. "If father leaves us in the forest again, we'll be able to follow the bits of bread all the way back home."

"You are clever, Hansel," said Gretel.

Once again, the woodcutter urged his children to rest as he began his work. They were so tired, they soon fell into a long sleep.

When the children woke up, they realized that their father had left them again. They were all alone in the cold, frightening forest.

"What are we going to do?" asked Gretel, nervously.

"We'll just follow the bits of bread, as I told you," Hansel replied, shivering a little from the cold. "Don't worry, everything will be fine." But as hard as they looked, the children couldn't find any pieces of bread, anywhere!

"Oh no!" cried Hansel. "The birds must have eaten it all. That's why we can't find any pieces of bread,"

That night, it was so cold it was impossible to keep still. The children walked around the forest, trying to keep warm, hoping that they wouldn't bump into a large, hungry animal. As the sun started to come up, they saw a white bird in the sky that seemed to be beckoning to them. Having no other plan, they followed the bird, which led them to a little cottage. They were amazed to see that the cottage walls were made entirely out of bread, the roof was iced ginger cake and the windows were made of sparkling sugar. Hansel and Gretel were so hungry they immediately began to tear bits of bread off the walls and ravenously started to eat it.

Just then, a little voice rang out:
"Nibble, nibble, little mouse,
Who's that nibbling at my house?"
Then the door opened and a little old lady came out. Hansel and Gretel thought they might be punished for eating bits of her house but the old lady simply smiled and said, "My goodness! You children must be hungry. Come inside and I'll make you breakfast."
The old lady seemed very kind, and made Hansel and Gretel a delicious breakfast.
Then she showed them to a tidy, little bedroom that had two comfortable beds in it, where they could have a lovely, long sleep.
"Aren't we lucky to have found this kind lady?" said Gretel as she got into bed.

But the kind old lady was not a kind old lady at all. She was, in fact, a horrible, nasty witch who enjoyed roasting children in her oven so that she could eat them!

The next morning, the cruel witch locked Hansel in a large cage with bars all around, and told Gretel to cook food for her brother.
"He needs fattening up before he's ready for my oven," she hissed to the poor girl.

Each day, the witch told Hansel to stick a finger through the bars so she could feel how fat he was getting. But Hansel was clever and, instead of poking out his finger, he stuck a little bone out, to make the witch think he wasn't putting on any weight at all!

After a month, the witch was getting impatient and decided to eat Hansel straight away. She ordered Gretel to make a fire in the oven, then told her to get into it to make sure it was hot enough. Poor Gretel knew that if she crawled into the oven, the witch would close the door behind her and roast her as well as her brother.

"I'm not very good at climbing into things. Could you show me how, please?" Gretel asked the witch.

"Oh, all right," said the witch, who opened the door and crawled inside the oven to show exactly how it should be done.

But, when the witch was halfway in, Gretel pushed her all the way with a great shove, and slammed the door shut behind her. And that was the end of a very horrible witch.

Gretel released her brother from the cage and together they searched the cottage for anything that might be useful. They were amazed to find that the cottage was crammed full of gold coins, silver trinkets and precious jewels. They gathered it all up and began to search for the way home.

After wandering for a long time, they saw smoke rising from a chimney in the distance. They were overjoyed to see that it was their cottage. They had found their home, at last.

When their father saw that his children were alive and well, he dropped his axe and hugged them close to him.

"I'm so happy to see you both again," he cried. "I thought you were dead, for sure!"

When he saw the treasure that they had brought with them, he couldn't believe his eyes.

Hansel and Gretel sold everything that they found in the witch's cottage and became very rich. Although their cruel mother had died while they were lost in the forest, the children and their father lived happily together for the rest of their days.

The Tinder Box

One day, a young soldier returning from the wars met an old woman on a lonely country road.

"Hello, young man," greeted the old woman, cheerily. "I've got a question for you. Tell me," she asked, would you like to take home with you as much money as you could carry?"

"Of course I would. Who wouldn't?" laughed the soldier.

"If you follow my instructions, you will be able to do just that," said the old woman.

The soldier was surprised by the woman's words but, having nothing better to do, decided to listen further.

First of all, the old woman took off her apron and gave it to the soldier. Then she told him that if he were to climb down into the hollow of the nearby tree, at the bottom he would find three doors. Behind the first door lay chests that were full of bronze coins, but there was a dog with eyes as big as saucers guarding them. If he lay the apron on the ground, the dog would sit on it and he could then stuff his pockets with the bronze coins.

Behind the second door was a room full of silver coins. There was also a dog guarding this room, and this dog had eyes as big as mill wheels! If he lay the apron on the ground again, this dog would also sit on it and he could take as many of the silver coins that he could carry.

The room behind the last door was full of gold coins, and the dog guarding these had eyes as big as towers! But, again, if the soldier lay the apron down, the dog would sit on it while he filled his pockets with the golden coins.

"This is all well and good," the soldier replied. "But nobody gives away treasure for nothing. What do you want in return?"

"The only thing I want is a small tinder box that lies in the room full of gold," the old woman replied.

The soldier agreed to bring her the tinder box. He then climbed down into the hollow of the tree, and, when he reached the bottom, it was exactly as the old woman had said. There were three doors directly in front of him. Behind the first door were chests full of bronze coins, and the dog with eyes as big as saucers was guarding them. The soldier placed the old woman's apron on the ground and the dog sat on it, just as she had said it would. He quickly stuffed his pockets full of the coins.

Behind the second door were chests full of silver coins, and guarding them was the dog with eyes as big as mill wheels. Again, the soldier lay the apron on the ground and the dog sat on it. Then the soldier emptied his pockets of all the bronze coins and filled them up with silver ones instead.

When he opened the last door, he gasped in astonishment. The room
was full of precious, gleaming gold coins. The dog guarding them looked
very fierce and really did have eyes as big as towers. The soldier once
more laid the apron down and the dog obediently sat on it. The soldier
then shook all of the silver coins out of his pockets and filled them up
again with as many gold coins as he could carry.

Remembering to pick up the tinder box that lay in the corner of the room, he then climbed out of the hollow tree.

"I see you've done very well for yourself," cackled the old woman, when she saw the soldier's pockets full of the gold coins. "But," she continued, "do you have the tinder box?"

"I most certainly do," replied the soldier. "However, before I give it to you, I would like to know why you want it so much."

"That is a secret," said the old woman.

"Then I will have to kill you and find out the secret for myself," he said. And, before she had a chance to say another word, he took out his sword and cut the old woman's head off.

Then, he put away his sword and went jauntily on his way.
Later that evening, the soldier reached a small town. With his pockets full of money, he stayed in the biggest room of the best inn and ordered the most expensive food and wine.
Over the next few months, he made lots of new friends and gave the most lavish parties.

But, eventually, the money ran out. His friends deserted him and he was forced to move to a cold, shabby attic. On his first night in the attic, he found an old candle which would at least give him a little heat and light. Remembering the old woman's tinder box, he struck it once to light it. There was a puff of smoke, and suddenly the dog with the eyes as big as saucers stood before him. The soldier was amazed to see the dog at first, but then thought he might be able to use him.

"Bring me some money!" ordered the soldier.

The dog disappeared, and soon returned with a bag full of bronze coins. When the soldier struck the tinder box twice, the dog with the eyes as big as mill wheels appeared. Once again, the soldier asked him for money, and this time the dog came back with a bag full of silver coins.

When the soldier struck the tinder box three times, the dog with eyes as big as towers appeared. When the soldier asked him for money, he returned with a bag full of gold coins.

The soldier was rich again! He moved into wonderful new lodgings, bought himself the most stylish clothes and lived a life of complete luxury.

One day, he saw the King's beautiful daughter pass by in her carriage. The soldier longed to meet her but was told that the King never let her out of his sight. So, one night, the soldier struck the tinder box again and, when the dog with eyes as big as saucers appeared, ordered him to bring the King's daughter to him. The dog did as he was told, carrying the sleeping Princess on his back. But a lady-in-waiting had followed the dog to the soldier's lodgings, and rushed to the palace to tell the King and Queen what she had seen.

The King and Queen were furious. When they found their daughter in the soldier's lodgings, they had him arrested immediately, and ordered that he be executed in the town square.

Early the next morning, the soldier was sitting in his cell, awaiting the dreaded hour, when a small boy's shoe fell through the bars from the street above.

"Can I have my shoe back, please?" asked the boy, peering through the bars.

"Certainly, you can," replied the soldier. "But only if you run to my lodgings and bring me my tinder box which is lying on the table."

The boy rushed off and, not long after, was wearing his shoe again. In his cell, the soldier sat staring at his tinder box with a smile on his face.

A few hours later the soldier was led up to the scaffold. When he was asked if he had a last request, he replied, "I'd like a final smoke of my pipe."

He put the pipe into his mouth and struck the tinder box once, then twice, then three times. There was a huge puff of smoke and all three dogs appeared, growling, at the soldier's side. On the soldier's order, they ran through the crowds towards the royal party.

The ferocious dogs killed the King and Queen where they stood and many of the courtiers and soldiers, too. Seeing how powerful he was, the people of the town freed the soldier and made him their new King. He married the old King's daughter the very next day.

The soldier was always protected by the three dogs, and lived a long life. He kept the tinder box hidden away in the castle vaults so no one would ever be able to take it away from him.

The Six Swans

In a land far, far away, there once lived a King with his six sons and a daughter. His children wanted for nothing in life. They studied with the best teachers, ate the finest food and wore only the most magnificent clothes. But, one day, the King married again. Unfortunately, the new Queen was an angry, bitter woman who hated her step-children on first sight. She decided to get rid of them all. First, she sent the young Princess away to live in the country and, not long after, cast an evil spell on the young Princes that turned them into six perfect, white swans.

"Go," she told them. "Fly far from here and find somewhere else to live."

When she was sixteen, the Princess was brought back to live in the palace. When the Queen saw how beautiful the Princess had become, the Queen became so jealous she smeared the poor girl's skin with walnut juice, tore her dress and made her hair look wild and tangled.

"Look at this peasant girl," cried the Queen, dragging the Princess by the hair to the King. "See how disgusting she looks. How can she be a King's daughter?"

The confused King agreed with his wife that the filthy girl standing in front of him could not possibly be his daughter, and ordered her to leave the palace at once.

The Princess walked into the nearby woods where she found a stream to bathe herself and wash away the foul walnut juice. She felt so lonely and sad, she began to cry. She longed to see her brothers again but had no idea where to find them.

As the sun began to set, and the lightness of the day turned into the darkness of the night, she looked up and saw six swans flying towards her. They flew lower and lower until they landed close to where the Princess stood. Then something strange happened. The swans began to change shape, shedding their feathers and turning into human form. With a gasp of astonishment, the Princess realized that the six swans had turned into her six long lost brothers.

The Princes told their sister that ever since they had been turned into
wild swans, they had lived in a far off land across the sea. They came
back to their homeland only once a year to fly over the palace where
they were born. They also told her that, although they were swans in
daylight, as soon as night fell, they turned back into human form again.
"At dawn we will change into swans, and fly back to the land where we
live. Will you come with us?" they asked their sister.
"I will," the Princess replied. "You are my brothers whom I love dearly.
I never want to be parted from you again."

That evening, the Princes worked hard, building a net of vine and willow bark that would carry the Princess. At first light, they turned back into swans and soared into the sky, bearing the weight of their sister between them. They flew for many hours without rest. The only thing the Princess saw was the glittering sea, below. But, as the day drew to its end and there were no signs of land, she began to worry. "It will soon be dark," she thought. "If we don't find land soon, my brothers will turn back into human form, and we will all fall into the sea and drown."

Shortly after, to her immense relief, the Princess saw land in the distance. Leaving the sea behind them, the swans set her down gently in a leafy forest glade. They turned back into the Princes again as soon as their feet touched the ground.

"Welcome to your new home," they said happily. That night the Princess had a dream. She dreamed that a wise old woman told her that her brothers could be freed and remain human if she were to collect a special nettle that grew in the forest. She had to weave the nettles into six magic cloaks which should be put around her brother's shoulders. Once this was done, the evil spell would be broken. But the old woman warned the Princess she must not speak until the cloaks were finished. If she uttered just one word, the cloaks would not work their magic. Early the next morning, convinced that the dream was an omen, the Princess started to gather the special nettles.

Later that day, the King of the land was out hunting, and noticed the Princess picking her nettles. He thought she was the most beautiful girl he had ever seen.
"Who are you?" he asked.

But, remembering the old lady's words, the Princess remained silent. The King was so enraptured by this beautiful, mute girl he decided to take her back to his palace with him and make her his Queen.

The whole country celebrated on the day of the marriage. Everyone, that is, except the King's Archbishop, who believed that the Princess was really a witch of the forest who had tricked the King into marrying her. "Of course she's a witch," the Archbishop thought to himself. "That's why she won't speak to anyone."

After she was married, the Princess continued her work on the magic cloaks in secret. One day, she ran out of the special nettles. That night she stole out of the palace and made her way to the forest, where she began to collect more. Unbeknown to her, the suspicious Archbishop had followed her. He rushed back to the King and told him what he had seen.
"I knew it all along!" cried the Archbishop. "The girl is collecting nettles to use in magic potions. She is a witch! She must be burned at the stake!" When faced with this charge the Princess, as ever, did not speak a word. The poor King loved his wife dearly but, in the face of the Archbishop's evidence, had little choice. With a heavy heart, he ordered that she must undergo a witch's punishment and be burned at the stake.

The Princess was dragged to the cells and, one week later, was taken by cart to the place of execution. As the cart made its way through the cobbled streets, the Princess worked furiously on the last of the special cloaks. As she neared the dreaded stake, there was a murmur from the crowd as six beautiful swans flew down and sat on the unlit bonfire. "This is an omen," some of the people whispered. "This surely means that our Queen is innocent!"

As the executioner reached for her hand to lead her up to the stake, the Princess quickly gathered up her nettle cloaks, jumped from the cart and threw them over the six swans. At once, the swans changed into the six handsome Princes. At last, they were free from the curse! They would never change into swans again.

"Now that my brothers are free, I can speak, my love," said the Princess to the King. When she told him the story of their stepmother's curse, the kindly King wept with pity for them.

"I nearly made a dreadful mistake," he said. "You and your brothers have shown much courage. I hope you will lead happier lives from now on. The Princes will always have my protection while they live in this land."

The brothers built palaces for themselves near to the royal palace. They visited their sister often and lived happily for the rest of their lives.

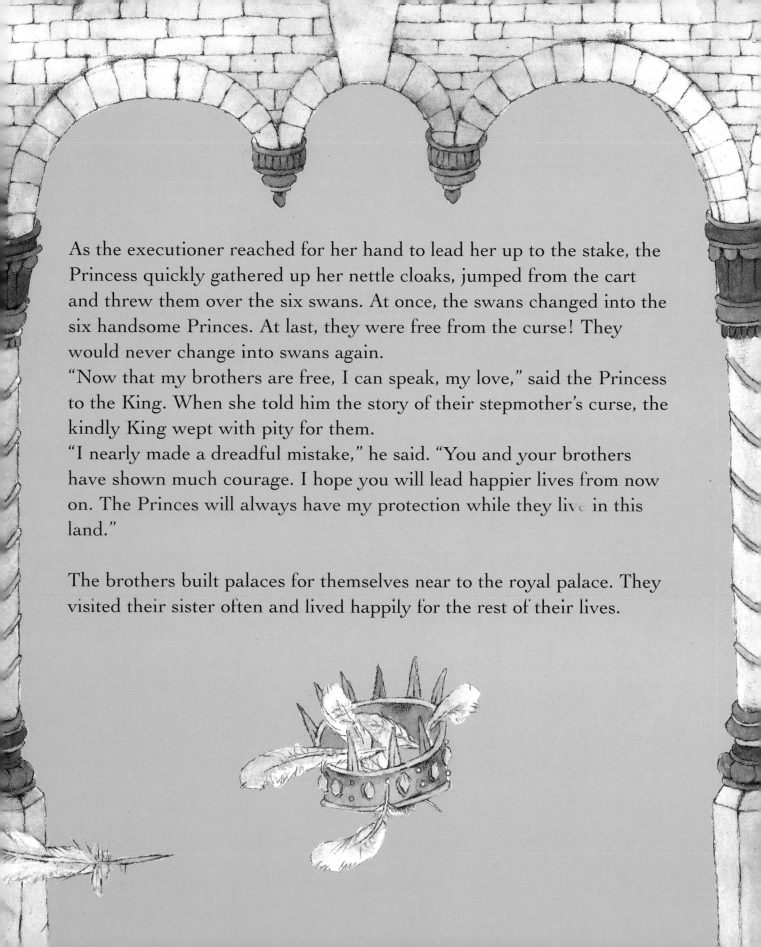

The Little Match Girl

It was New Year's Eve. Everyone in the city was scurrying through the freezing cold snow to get home as quickly as possible. Everyone, that is, except the poor little match girl. She could not move quickly. She had no shoes and her little feet were turning blue from the cold. Soon, they would be frozen, and she wouldn't be able to walk at all.

She hobbled along as far as she could then, seeing a sheltered doorway, stopped to rest. Earlier in the day, she had lost her mother's slippers that she'd been wearing. Being far too big for her, the slippers had fallen off as she'd been running across a busy road, and a passing carriage had run over them. They were completely ruined, so she had worked all day in her bare feet, trying to sell her matches. In all her short life, she had never felt as bitterly cold as this.

True, she had a roof over her head, but the walls of the tiny house she lived in were thin, and had cracks so large that in winter, icy winds constantly blew through them. Anyway, it was impossible to go home yet. Her father, who didn't care for anyone or anything, would beat her if she didn't bring back some money. And she hadn't sold a match all day.

She blew on her frozen hands, trying to get a little warmth into them. If only she could light a match. That would be lovely.

The match would spark up and its flame would glow bright orange, inviting her hands to get as close to it as possible. Then, some of its heat would seep through to her freezing fingers for a few seconds before the flame burned itself out.

Oh, yes . . . that would be lovely! But what would her father do to her if she wasted a match in that way?

She looked around. The street was empty now. No one was there to see her crime and, besides, she didn't care any more what her father would do to her. She needed the warmth and comfort that the flame would bring. It was some time before her frozen fingers managed to get a match out of the box but, eventually, she managed it. The flame roared into life, lighting up the poor girl's haggard face.

Then something strange happened. A splendid scene of a roaring fire in a warm, cosy room appeared before her. If only she could stretch out her feet a little, surely the fire would warm them right through. But as she began to stretch out her toes, the match went out, and the room and the glowing fire disappeared with the flame.

She lit another match. This time, it was as though the match had turned the solid wall next to her into thin gossamer, and she could see right through it to the room beyond. She saw a large table groaning under the weight of beautiful, fine china and hot, delicious food. A big dish of roast potatoes steamed away, surrounded by smaller dishes filled with vegetables, stuffing and gravy. There was a massive chocolate cake covered in rich, sticky icing and, right in the middle of the table, sat a fine, roasted goose. The little match girl had never seen such delights. She tried to reach out and touch it. But as soon as she moved her hand towards the feast, the match spluttered and died. All that remained was the solid brick wall.

She lit a third match, hoping to see all the food again. But this time she found herself in a beautiful room sitting at the foot of a magnificent Christmas tree with hundreds of candles shining brightly on it. It seemed to the little match girl that all the candles were rising slowly into the air, lighting up the sky for miles. But then she saw that the candles weren't really candles at all. They were really stars twinkling in the heavens. She noticed that one of the stars had started to fall slowly away.

"When a star falls, a soul is going up to God," her grandmother used to tell her. Her grandmother had died some years before and the little match girl missed her dearly. She was the only person in her short life who had truly loved her.

She lit another match and rubbed her eyes in disbelief! Her grandmother was standing right in front of her, smiling at her from the middle of the flame. But, all too soon, the flame died out and the poor little girl was alone once more.

"No!" she cried. "I want to see my granny again."
She took a handful of matches and struck them all together. A huge flame lit up and her grandmother appeared again. This time, closer than ever.
"Oh, granny," cried the little match girl. "I am so miserable here. I want to be with you."
"And you will be, my child," said her grandmother, kindly. She reached out and gathered her granddaughter into her arms and held onto her tightly as they rose ever higher into the blazing sky.

The next morning, the frozen body of the little match girl was found in a shop's doorway. Scattered all around her dead body were the blackened ends of burnt out matches.
"Poor little mite tried to keep herself warm," someone said, sadly.
No one would ever know of the wonderful visions that the little match girl had seen that night, or how gloriously the angels sang when she and her grandmother rose up to God and entered the Kingdom of Heaven.

The Emperor's New Clothes

Many years ago, there lived an Emperor. He was a very nice Emperor and kind to lots of people, but he secretly believed that no one really respected him. He thought he was a, bald, fat, silly little man who wasn't grand and important at all.

However much his wife tried to tell him everyone admired him, he refused to believe it. To try to make himself look as important as possible, he started to spend a lot of time choosing exactly the right clothes to wear. He always hired the best tailors, and made sure they used only the finest material.

The Emperor's passion for clothes grew and grew, and became widely known throughout his Empire. He had a huge room in his palace containing rows of beautiful gowns. Another room was stuffed full of different uniforms, and a third room had rolls and rolls of the most exquisite cloth piled high to the ceiling.

When he got out of bed, he would put on a magnificent silk dressing gown. After bathing, he would change into one of his many attractive robes for eating breakfast. After breakfast, he would change into something formal to discuss important matters with his ministers. Then he would change into something less formal in which to have lunch. On and on it went until, by the time he went to bed again, he'd changed his clothes more times in a day than most people would in a week!

One day, a clever swindler, pretending to be a tailor, came to see the Emperor.

"Your Majesty," began the swindler. "If you allow me to, I can make you the finest set of clothes ever seen."

These words immediately held the Emperor's interest.

"The finest clothes ever seen!" he exclaimed, excitedly.

"Yes, your Majesty," said the swindler. "In fact, these clothes are so special, they are invisible to anyone who is a complete and utter fool. Look, let me show you the cloth I'm going to use."

The swindler took precisely nothing out of his case and proceeded to show it to the Emperor.

"See how fine it is," enthused the swindler.

Not wanting to seem a complete and utter fool, the Emperor had to agree that the cloth did, indeed, look wonderful.

The Emperor told the swindler to start making his new clothes straight away, because he wanted to wear them at the next month's royal procession. The swindler was given a room of his own in the palace where he could get on with his work. Whenever anyone passed by, they could always hear through the closed door the furious whirring of his sewing machine.

After two weeks, the Emperor ordered his Prime Minister to see how his new clothes were coming along.

The Prime Minister knocked on the swindler's door.

"May I come in?" he asked. "His Excellency wishes to know how you're getting on with his new clothes."

"Of course, sir," said the swindler, opening the door.

"There's still a lot of work to do, sir," said the swindler. "But I think you'll agree that the Emperor will not be disappointed."

And, with a great flourish, he draped the new clothes along his arm for the Prime Minister to admire.

"Oh, yes. They look … well … absolutely wonderful!" said the Prime Minister, too embarrassed to say that he was looking at precisely nothing!

There was great excitement in the palace on the day of the procession. The Emperor couldn't wait to get into his new outfit, and paced nervously up and down his dressing room.

"I hope the people like me in my new clothes," he thought. "And I hope they make me look as strong and important as an Emperor should look."

When they finally arrived, the Emperor took his dressing gown off, put the new clothes on and paraded up and down in them.

"Magnificent!" exclaimed the swindler.

"You look so dignified!" gasped the Prime Minister.

"Yes, I do, don't I?" said the Emperor, rather grandly, prancing up and down in front of the mirror. "Today," he announced nobly, "I shall look like a real Emperor!"

Many people had crowded the streets in order to get a good look at the Emperor in his magnificent new clothes.

"Here he comes!" one of them yelled, spotting the Emperor stepping out of the palace.

"Doesn't he look wonderful!" exclaimed everyone, also not wishing to look foolish.

The men in the crowd bowed, and the women curtsied deeply as the Emperor passed by.

"I feel so powerful in my new clothes!" thought the Emperor, parading through the streets with his head held high.

Suddenly, a little boy stepped out from the crowd, pointed at the Emperor, and shouted:

"Wait a minute … he hasn't got any clothes on!"

There was a huge gasp from the crowd, then everyone fell silent. All of a sudden, someone tittered, another giggled, and soon everyone was laughing hysterically at their Emperor who stood before them as naked as the day he was born.

The poor Emperor had never been so humiliated in his life. He turned the brightest red, and wished the ground would open up and swallow him. Then an unusual thing happened. Instead of running away in embarrassment, he lifted his chin and began to walk grandly through the streets again. From somewhere deep inside him, the Emperor had found the courage that he'd always felt he'd lacked.

"Look at that!" said the crowd. "As naked as a newborn baby, but walking through our streets like a lion! What a man! Long Live the Emperor!"

After the procession, the Emperor rushed back to his palace. He realized he didn't need fine garments to make him feel grand and important anymore, so he gave away most of his beautiful clothes. At long last, he felt grand and important within himself. Which is just how an Emperor should feel.

The Selfish Giant

nce upon a time there was a giant who came down into the valley from his home in the mountains and built himself a castle with a beautiful garden. The giant was very proud of his new garden and all the lovely things in it. He especially liked spring, when all the pretty new flowers came out, the shrubs blossomed and a warm breeze blew through the branches in his many trees, softly rattling the leaves.

On spring days such as this, the giant liked nothing better than to open his window and hear the sound of the local children playing in his garden. They came very early in the morning, and played there the whole day until it was getting dark and time to go home.
"See you tomorrow," they waved to the giant, who gave his funny, toothless grin and waved slowly back.

One year, the giant decided to return to the mountains to visit his only friend, Horace. Horace was a giant too, and lived so high up in the mountains, it was completely barren and nearly always cold. While he was there, Horace told the gentle giant that he was foolish to let all the children play in his garden.
"I know you," said Horace, taking a big mouthful of apple pie. "You're too soft with those children. You'll let them run around until they have trampled all of your flowers! You mark my words, if you let them play in there all of the time, they will ruin your precious garden!"

The giant thought long and hard about this and came to the conclusion that Horace was right. From that moment on, his heart began to harden. "Those children don't care anything at all for my garden," he thought. "They're just using it to have fun in. Once they've ruined it, they'll just go and find somewhere else to play!"

This thought made him feel very angry. The very next day, he packed his things, said goodbye to Horace and, with his huge strides, walked back down the mountain to his castle.

Once he arrived, he opened his gate and saw all the children enjoying themselves as usual.

"Get out of my garden!" he yelled at them in his big, booming voice. "Go on, get out! You're not welcome here anymore!"

The children were very frightened. They had never seen the giant angry before, and they ran away as quickly as they could. As soon as they were gone, the giant began to build a huge wall around his garden so no one could get in. When the wall was finished, he made a sign and nailed it to the garden gate. The sign read: Private Property! Keep Out! Then he took a key out of his pocket and locked the gate.

"That's that," he said, with a satisfied look on his face, and took himself off to bed.

The next day, it started to get much colder. Winter had arrived, and with it the hail, ice and snow. But when spring came around again, and the birds began to sing and the flowers started to bloom, it was still winter inside the giant's garden. When the giant looked out of his window, he couldn't understand why winter had stayed. He missed seeing the lovely flowers and hearing the birds who nested in his trees, and he became very sad.

Years passed, and the seasons came and went, but nothing changed inside the giant's garden. It was cold and bleak, and nothing would grow. Once, when a small flower peeked its head above the ground, it quickly went back down again when it saw that the giant's garden was so unwelcoming.

One day, some children were passing by and wondered what lay behind the huge wall. They made a small hole and crawled through the wall into the garden. Each child climbed a tree, laughing and joking as they went higher and higher. When the giant pulled back his curtains, a big grin spread across his face. His garden was beautiful again! All the flowers were out, the grass was green and luscious, the bees were busy buzzing but, best of all, he heard the laughter of excited children high up in the trees, throwing blossom over themselves.

"Spring has finally returned!" he cried, and rushed outside.

But in the farthest corner of the garden, the giant saw a sad sight. A little boy was crying because he wasn't tall enough to climb a tree. Seeing the boy so upset, melted the giant's heart. He reached down, picked the boy up and gently sat him in the branches of a tree.

"I've been so selfish, not allowing the children to play in my garden," he thought. "No wonder winter wanted to stay."

But when the other children saw him, they became scared and started to run away.

"Don't go," pleaded the giant. "This is your garden now. Look!"

Then he fetched the biggest axe he could find and knocked down the wall down until it was nothing but dust.

When the people of the town passed by, they couldn't believe what they saw. The giant was enjoying himself! He was lying in the middle of the garden, laughing uncontrollably as the children clambered and played all over him.

From that day on, the children came to play in the giant's garden whenever they could. Often, the giant would play with them and, in the warm evenings, tell them stories of his ancestors who had never been out of the mountains.

As the giant got older, it became more difficult for him to move around, so he liked to sit in his big armchair by the window, watching the children playing in the garden.

"What a stupid giant I was before," he'd think, "building a wall that kept me away from all this happiness. Thank goodness I realized my mistake."

Then he'd shut his eyes and, with the sound of children's laughter ringing in his ears, he'd fall into a long, contented sleep.